# SOPHIE'S DREAM

Sophie dreams of an exciting life away from her strict education in a workhouse. Through an agency she applies for a position as a Governess in New South Wales in Australia. She is chaperoned, with other young women, to a new life, beyond the social barriers in England. But Sophie finds that the agency is a sham when she's abandoned on the quayside in Sydney. However, a different world opens up to her when she meets Mr Matthias Wells . . .

VALERIE HOLMES

# SOPHIE'S DREAM

*Complete and Unabridged*

# LINFORD
*Leicester*

First published in Great Britain in 2012

First Linford Edition
published 2012

British Library CIP Data

Holmes, Valerie.
 Sophie's dream.- -(Linford romance library)
 1. Love stories.
 2. Large type books.
 I. Title II. Series
 823.9'2–dc23

 ISBN 978–1–4448–0993–0

Published by
F. A. Thorpe (Publishing)
Anstey, Leicestershire

Set by Words & Graphics Ltd.
Anstey, Leicestershire
Printed and bound in Great Britain by
T. J. International Ltd., Padstow, Cornwall

This book is printed on acid-free paper

# 1

Sophie looked along the length of the barque to Mr Simmons. He was leaning against the rails staring eagerly toward the direction of the new land. The other young women who had left England with their group all stood around him, bracing themselves as best they could against the sway of the moving vessel. Their faces showed a spread of emotions, from fear to relief at nearing solid ground. None but Sophie had eyes filled with anticipation of a future she wanted to enjoy and grab in both hands.

Mr Simmons had acted as her guardian throughout this long voyage, along with the other young women who he had recruited in Yorkshire. Their journey had begun in a simple office in Harrogate. From there, once accepted, they and their references had been vetted and travel arrangements made; they had been taken by coach to Whitby where they joined a packet to London and had stayed one exciting night in a small hotel. Early the next morning they had been taken by coach to the south coast. That had been the furthest Sophie had ever travelled in her life. Now here she was approaching a shore on the other side of the world. A grin appeared on her face; Sophie's dream was coming true.

She stood slightly apart from the group. The rest, looking anxiously on as they viewed the strange land coming into view, clung to Mr Simmons as children to their mama, but Sophie braced herself, standing independently, one hand on her bonnet anticipating life in New South Wales. She felt the swell of the ocean as the ship changed direction, turning toward the harbour, and knew that on these shores she faced the challenge of making her future her own: Freedom from the old constraints of a childhood as an orphan left at the workhouse and, more recently, from the farm where she had been sent at the age of twelve. There Sophie had run in open country, worked in fields, breathed fresh air and lived and loved working alongside the animals whenever she could escape the chores of the house. Now she had her dream, and an opportunity to make her own way in life, one where her past would not matter because here the old rules would not apply.

Sophie felt moisture on her cheeks. Wiping it away she convinced herself that it was no more than the spray from the sea, but she knew it was a momentary lapse of foolish emotion. She had nothing in England to pine for, no one there to care about. Sophie was free to make what she could of her new life and her position. There were nerves fluttering in her stomach at the prospect of being a housekeeper in a captain's house. She would have to make sure that she was equal to the task. After all, she had not lied when she had applied at the office in Grove Street, and they had seemed happy with her reference from Mrs Peters at the home, and Reverend Boddie who had given her a note of good character at the request of the Cuthbertsons, the farming family she had lived and worked with for five years. So why should she doubt her decision and her actions now?

She glanced along the side of the barque; the three masts glimmered and the square rigging moved as sailors busied themselves pulling ropes as they were shouted orders. It all fascinated Sophie, but she understood little of their world. She was glad to be leaving this wallowing ship; she had seen too much ocean, the constant roll and pitch of the swell becoming monotonous. How she longed to take up her new position in a house with a bedroom of her own, instead of lying in her space separated only by hung curtains from the other women. One hundred and eleven days of perpetual motion would soon end with her, Sophie Dove, stepping into a new and exciting world. She smiled again.

Sophie watched the other girls standing by Mr Simmons. A niggling doubt of uncertainty spoiled her moment of optimism. She had seen them in the depth of despair in a storm, on the brink of melancholia after the sickness had hit them as they left Plymouth harbour, and now the shadows of doubt still lingered upon them. Mercy looked the more confident, she thought. They did not seem to be very 'ladylike', she knew Matilda could cook, Maud sought to find a husband, but neither Dora, Thea or Mercy seemed to have any training at all and had not learned their letters. It seemed a long way to bring general house maids. Still they would also find husbands, no doubt. Sophie held the rail and smiled into the sun and breeze. She was not here to find a 'keeper'. With her new position she was here to learn and grow. If she could save her earnings, she may even start a business of her own — a woman equal to a man. If this new land was to be different in any way then that one way should be how this new world viewed women.

She almost bit her lip with excitement as the harbour of Port Arthur came into view once the ship had negotiated Sydney Cove. The land was so different to that she had left behind. Two headlands loomed and then the sounding of a gun firing announced their arrival. Strange birds lifted high into the sky, disturbed by the noise, but she did not care if they were strange and different, because that was what she craved. Dark trees, not like the oaks of home, gave way to a settlement.

'You scared, Missie Yani?'

The voice, slightly nervous, snapped her attention back from her dreams and observations. She looked down to where her secret friend was squatted behind a curled up rope. Most of the ship's crew were coarse and their group of women had been kept very much separate from them so there was no chance of a relationship of any standing forming between them and the men. Even the officers were kept at a distance with Mr Simmons keeping a watchful eye on his little group. The young lad, a native to these shores, had been her only friend as she had given him some of the food from their table: the odd piece of bread, and an apple in the early part of the voyage. He seemed ill at ease with the men and worked hard and was often cruelly kicked out of their way when scrubbing decks. He was not a willing seaman.

'It looks as beautiful as you described it, Dorak,' she whispered, knowing that if he was found talking to her he would be beaten and she severely chastised. In fact, the crew thought him to be dumb, ignorant, but Dorak was far more knowledgeable than they could have imagined.

'Why do you call me Yani?' she said, as she turned her head away from the direction of Mr Simmons for fear he would suspect something. The crew were too busy at their tasks and scouting the land to notice what she was doing.

'Means peace, Missie — is what you are.'

He was huddled as far back as he could get. So small and vulnerable, she thought. She wondered how old he really was. 'That is lovely. No one has ever said kinder words to me. I shall treasure them always. So what does Dorak mean?'

'Lively!'

She glanced down and could see he was grinning up at her. She wanted to tell him to stand by her and watch his homeland appear. To ask him hundreds of questions all about surviving in this strange land, but then he vanished silently into the shadows and she knew he had gone.

'When we disembark, Miss Dove, you will need to stay with the group. Make sure you have your bag with you. This is a beautiful but dangerous place and you need to be close to me at all times until we can ascertain if your new employer has made arrangements for your transport. I hold your references and shall, with the other young ladies, escort you to our office. We call it the 'sorting room' as we make sure everyone's paperwork is in order and that the correct lady leaves with their new employer. I have written a letter to the Reverend Boddie informing him of your safe arrival and happiness in your new home, so that the Cuthbertsons will not worry about you. It will return on the next ship out.'

'That is very thoughtful of you, Mr Simmons,' Sophie answered, thinking him very efficient, but knowing they thought her mad for coming out to such a place as a 'foreign' country in the first place. They expected her to die of fever. She knew this because it was the final warning she had heard as she left their farmhouse. Her work would be missed, no doubt, if not her.

'You have shown a certain indepen-dence of character throughout your journey, which may hold you in good stead as your start your new life, but down there . . . ' he gestured to the port as it came closer into view, and her initial impression of buildings and trees that Dorak had told her was what white men called Eucalyptus trees, gave way to the vision of soldiers, working convict men, inns and dockworkers. 'Down there, is a very dangerous place for a young lady to be on her own. Stay close to me, do not question strangers or wander from my protection and remain silent until we are in the sorting room where all will be explained. You do not want to draw unwelcome attention to yourself. I will see your journey completed as I pass you into the right hands, so to speak.' He stared at her, waiting for her response.

'Yes, of course, Mr Simmons. I was just taking the fresh air after what has been an exhausting journey.' She smiled at him. She had in fact taken more air than the rest of the ladies. Dora and Maud had slumped into the lowest spirits on leaving Plymouth's sheltered harbour. Matilda and Mercy had watched the sailors and the officers when they had any chance to from the moment they had stepped aboard the ship. Mr Simmons warned them of the sin of lust. That had calmed them down for a time, but their eyes wandered often over the men through the weeks and months that had passed by aboard the ship. Her stomach had attuned itself earlier than theirs to the motion of the mass of water beneath the vessel as its moods changed like the wind. Dorak had given her a drink when he found her being ill one night. She had drunk it without hesitation; that trust shown had touched him and a tentative friendship had formed. Forbidden, but as he put it, 'two lost souls sharing a troubled journey'. Mercy seemed to have formed a closer friendship with Mr Simmons than anyone else in the group, as she listened to him the most.

'Good. Remember that, child; an independent spirit in a female is not desirable here anymore than it is in our dear homeland.' The warning in his words was almost tangible.

'Of course, I understand perfectly, Mr Simmons,' she repeated, and stared ashore. Not wanting to look into the man's pale eyes. The uneasiness which had been growing within her re-emerged. The barque bumped alongside as it was secured. They had arrived, and the ship was a hive of activity.

Eventually, they all walked onto the new country's soil. It felt strange, to be standing on something that was static; her legs wanted to keep moving. Mr Simmons led their party, then Mercy followed on, whilst the others, as if all were behind their mother bird, tagged along like ducklings; lastly, Sophie followed carrying her bag.

Mr Simmons rushed forward as if looking for someone. He ventured to a building which had a door sealed up with a plank of wood on which a notice had been pinned. He did not stay to make sure that his group stayed together. The door was locked and the windows were boarded up. He seemed to be reading the notice on the door. Then, without saying a word to them, he looked left and right. Sophie could see many soldiers around the dock, some in charge of the chained convict gangs, others falling in and out of inns further around the quay. Yet more were meeting the ship, some wanting news from home, others eyeing all new arrivals. Two had seen Mr Simmons and appeared to be walking in his direction. Strangely, he turned the other way and increased his speed as he strode off.

The women had grouped as they had been told to, but seeing Mr Simmons walking off they decided to follow him. Sophie stopped and turned back to look at the ship which her life had depended upon for so long. She was not wallowing in any sort of nostalgia but for a little sad face. Sad herself that she could not see her friend to wave goodbye to him and wish him well, she turned to join her group. She was shocked to see that they had moved off at a pace, apparently trying to keep up with Mr Simmons who appeared to be striding ahead without intention of looking back at them. Something was wrong, she sensed it. So Sophie stood and watched, waiting for her instinct to tell her what to do next. She put her hand in her pocket and pulled out the cutting with the address of the offices of 'Cambridge Recruitment Agency: Securers of positions for ladies of good character and training.'

So where were they? Why was their representative not here so that they could be met?

# 2

The whitewashed buildings of the township had looked so pretty and clean from the ship with the smell of salt in the air, but standing here, the towns filth was clear to see and smell. The grime and stink reminded her of the docks where the barque had departed from in England. Sophie saw a line of convicts hobbled together, chained by the wrists, shuffling along the harbour side in the charge of soldiers. It reminded her of slavery. Surely there should be a more generous way of correcting the deeds of the desperate, for in her childhood she had seen the suffering of broken men and women in the workhouse. From the dormitory window she had even glimpsed the silent figures of men breaking rocks in the yard. The silence except from the strokes of their mallets had been awful to her. Their faces had been crushed by the tedium and hardship, spirits as broken as the rocks they assaulted.

Sophie moved her bag over to where crates were stacked at the side of a warehouse building. Here she felt out of their way. The men looked thin, bedraggled, and their eyes lifeless. Were these the reformed characters that the government boasted of back home? She saw something move behind the crates and nearly let out a scream, but she heard the voice just in time.

'Bye, missie.'

Dorak's smile appeared as she heard his familiar voice, but then her attention was taken by a group of sailors running along the quay in her direction carrying musket and clubs. They stopped short of her as one shouted out to the soldiers.

'Seen a black fella running this way?'

'No, mate, sorry. I'll keep me eyes open. He stole summit?' one soldier asked.

'He's a runaway,' the sailor answered,

but his attention had moved on. He now looked in her direction.

Sophie knew Dorak was still hiding behind her nestled into the gap between the crates. He could not go further until the chain gang passed by.

'You seen 'im?' the man shouted to her; his manner as gruff as his appearance.

'No, perhaps he went that way.' She pointed towards the harbour buildings in the opposite direction. One of the sailors let his club swing loosely in his hand as he approached Sophie.

'You look lost, miss. Perhaps Evan could help you find a place to lay your head. Settle in like?' he smiled at her, showing a mixture of browning chipped teeth.

'I am not lost and I do not think I need your assistance,' she said as boldly as she dared. Mr Simmons was nowhere in sight. The group of women appeared to have been split up. Matilda and Mercy were talking openly and animatedly to two officers, whilst Thea, Dora and Maud were being escorted by two gentlemen into a side door of the building opposite the closed office where Mr Simmons had tried to enter. It looked like an inn. Mr Simmons was nowhere to be seen.

'Hey, Bart, look at this. A lady has arrived all on her ownsome and does not need us men folk to come to her aid. I think she needs to learn a few laws of the land. Or perhaps she'd prefer it, if she is too good for the inns that is, we could ask yonder soldiers to take her for a visit to the female factory, and then she might reconsider her options. They'd like her in there, all pretty and fresh.'

His friend chuckled. The soldiers smiled, but were too busy with their unfortunate charges to join in the man's taunts.

'I am well familiar with the law . . . '

'Oh, I'd like you to be familiar with me . . . ' the man was almost in front of her. She prayed that he would not see Dorak. Fear for his situation was now being overtaken by the realisation she

18

was also being overcome by fear for herself.

'The lady said she had no need of your help.' The voice, cold, determined and challenging came from behind her. She was as shocked as Dorak when the stranger spoke to the sailor from the shadows of the building behind them.

The sailor raised his club. 'Come out, you coward, and say that again.'

Sophie glanced back. She could see Dorak out of the corner of her eye, stock still, eyes wide, ready to break for freedom given the chance, but the man who had spoken came forward with his rifle pointed at the sailor, who instantly dropped the club to hang loosely by his side again and started backing away.

'Now, mister, no need to be like that, we was only being friendly, trying to help the young miss.' He rejoined his friends and they headed off toward the main harbour buildings in search of their prey, hardly glancing back.

Sophie looked at the gentleman who had helped her: tall, well dressed in a coat that resembled a greatcoat, wearing a wide-brimmed hat. He looked at her from beneath his ebony coloured fringe whilst holding his rifle across his body, his arms casually crossed.

She glanced anxiously at Dorak.

The stranger looked directly at him, waiting for the last of the convicts to pass. Sophie realised he had seen her lie to cover this boy's escape bid.

'Kut — ti!' the man said, quietly, but firmly.

'Mur — rom — boo' the boy replied, nodding his thanks to Sophie, then in a blink of an eye he had disappeared into the shadows of the building and vanished.

'They will bring you trouble, miss. Stay away from them.' He looked at Sophie, nodded and then turned as if to walk away, no more to be said.

'My thanks also,' she said, and followed a step behind him carrying her bag. 'Were you warning me to stay away from young native boys or grown sailors who should know better than to pick on young females?' she asked.

He turned and looked at her curiously. 'You know what those words meant?'

Sophie nodded. 'He taught me a few local words whilst we were on the ship.' She gestured towards the barque. As her eyes met his stare, she blushed. She had just admitted, so easily to this stranger, that she had talked to the lad on the journey here. Sophie realised that she was now an unchaperoned lady standing on a dockside talking to a complete stranger who was carrying a rifle. However, Sophie had spent a lifetime being on her own, whilst surrounded by people. She had learnt to obey rules made by people who had their own social etiquette, these were luxuries the poor were not afforded. Standing here, Sophie tried to look confident, despite the growing doubts which filled her mind as to what she should do next.

'Both, stay away from both. You will bring trouble to the lad and his kind if you consort with them and destroy your own reputation, and the sailors will definitely bring trouble to you. Good day, miss.' He took a pace forward towards the township.

'Perhaps you could help me,' she persisted, seeing that the officers were now escorting Matilda and Mercy into the barrack block.

'Perhaps I could not.' He did not stop.

The sharpness of his words almost stung. 'Sir . . . I . . . '

This time he paused and glanced back at her. Holding his rifle in his right hand, his left cupped her elbow as he took her to the side of the warehouse so that an ox and dray could pass by unheeded.

'Miss, without wishing to offer offence I will speak plainly. I am not looking to find a wife or a woman . . . I merely purchase supplies and shall leave this place tomorrow morning.'

Sophie stared up into his sun-kissed face. He had lost the paleness of the

Europeans and had a gentle tan — not hard and lined like the poor convicts whose faces were not shielded by the wide brim of a hat, but an even tan on what she guessed was younger skin than she had first thought. His eyes that had burned so deep when he stood up to the sailor showed a hint of softness now as he spoke to her, trying to let her down tactfully. She wanted to laugh openly at his arrogance, but resisted. Sophie realised she needed his help. Her situation was not going well. Sophie had to think quickly and carefully for, whatever this stranger was in life, he was no man — or woman's fool, of that she was certain.

She could not stop a smile breaking through and saw his expression change instantly. The stranger's look of arrogant assumption was being replaced by a look of genuine bewilderment.

'That is just as well, sir, because I am not looking for a husband or a man. I am looking for the offices of this establishment,' she spoke quickly and held out a piece of paper to him. It was her letter of introduction, 'so that I may meet my new employer. I have attained a position of housekeeper to a captain.' She unfolded it, wishing that she had not allowed Mr Simmons to take her references.

He took the paper in his hand and looked at it, studying it carefully.

'The position being in the household of a Captain D. J. Locker?'

She smiled and nodded. 'Yes, do you know him?'

He sighed. 'How old are you, miss?' His face looked almost reconciled to being stuck with her for at least as long as it would take to fulfil this introduction — she hoped.

'I do not think that is a suitable question to ask a lady, sir,' she answered, standing as tall as she could whilst trying to look severe, as she had been told that would make her look more mature than she was.

'How old?'

'Twenty one, sir' she blushed. Her

attention turned back to the ship. She could feel his stare, hoping he would accept this as the truth and not push her on the subject. She preferred to avoid outright lies and just manipulate the truth now and then, but this man was direct in his manner.

He tipped his hat back on his head with his finger and half smiled at her. 'How old-the truth or I will leave you to those wolves over there.'

Sophie saw his hand gesture towards a group of soldiers leaving an inn.

She did not like his attitude and thought for a moment of insisting, but then he started to look away as if he meant to leave her. His features were as strong as his eyes were dark. He had inner-strength of character and Sophie believed he would do whatever he said he would, but he had also helped Dorak and spoke the boy's tongue, so he was more charitable than the men she had encountered on the voyage so far, including Mr Simmons. Her hardened stranger had a softer side.

'Nineteen,' she spoke quietly. 'But I am equal to the task and shall make Captain Locker proud of his home!' This statement came out with confidence for she believed it to be true.

'Let me show you something.' He picked up her bag and walked her over to the door to read the notice that Mr Simmons had previously read and apparently run away from.

She read the note. It was brief. It said

'To all young ladies arriving to report to the premises of the 'Cambridge Recruitment Agency' be warned. This establishment is now closed and all arrivals should report to the barracks forthwith.'

She looked at the stranger. 'Where are the barracks? Would you escort me there and perhaps they can arrange for me to go to the captain's home?'

Instead, he walked her around the corner of the wooden building, along the narrow street and away from the main road.

'The establishment was closed because it was false — a honey trap to attract single, young girls with no families.'

'How do you know I have no family?' she asked.

'None of them did. No one to ask questions when they 'disappeared'. No one to write home to. You are very fortunate that their policy was to bring you out here untouched, as it were.'

'How dare you say such things!' she began to protest. 'Do you think that I am the sort of woman who would consort with . . .'

'Lady . . . girl, the moment you stepped on board that ship you lost control of your life.'

'I took control of it. I came here to make a better life. Mr Simmons was our chaperone and . . .'

He raised a hand to stop her talking. 'Your Mr Simmons has taken to his heels because if he is caught he will be arrested and thrown in irons. His job

27

was to bring you safely to this office. You would have then been gathered in a room . . . '

'Yes, the sorting room where we were introduced to our new employers. He explained this to me before we disembarked.' Sophie looked at this sceptical man defiantly.

'Where you would have been sorted surely enough and bid for. Your future determined as a wife, woman or whore; coin would have passed hands and your future sealed. They wanted a higher bidding price so you were escorted here safely; no doubt they were hoping that officers would be interested. Other girls have not been so lucky and that is a very long voyage. You, miss, have been lucky, so far. However, your captain does not exist.' He almost whispered these last words as he brought his head down to hers as if willing the implications to sink in.

'You are certain of this?' Sophie hated feeling defeated. She was not stupid and realised the truth in his words, but she knew he was somehow her way out of this mess, for Sophie believed in fate and that God placed people in a person's path at times when they were most needed. That was, if you asked, and Sophie asked often.

'Captain D. J. Locker — Captain Davey Jones Locker, perhaps.'

'Fool!' she snapped.

He looked taken aback.

'Not you, me and Mercy, Thea, Maud, Matty and Dora. We must find them. We must warn them . . . we must save them before it is too late . . . ' She walked briskly toward the main road.

'Stop! We can not undo what will have already been done. They have already succumbed to their path by going off with the men who propositioned them. Which leaves you on your own, miss. There are many men here, some are good, and who still need wives. You could do worse than find yourself one. They advertise and . . . '

'And nothing!' Sophie came back to him. 'I did not come here to sell my body in any way not even into wedlock; I came to carve out a future for myself.'

He almost smiled. She was not certain if he was silently laughing at her or her position, but she was not going to be defeated at the first thing to go awry. Even Sophie had to admit that this time things had gone badly wrong, but then looking at the sunny side of the cloud, which she always tried to do, she was still as she was when she left England. She could still turn her fortunes around, if only the stranger would help her to see how.

'You have spirit, take care; you will need every ounce of it.' He walked past her carrying her bag.

Sophie tried to keep in step with him. 'Where are we going?'

'I am going to my hotel. You are going to see if they need any maids. Or you could go to the barracks, but I would strongly advise against it.' He kept walking.

'Why? Are soldiers not to be trusted here either?' she asked and was rewarded by a laugh as he glanced down at her.

'You are not so dim. So your head is not turned by a pretty uniform?'

'No, sir, it is not.'

'Good, keep it that way. They make the law, they are the law.' His smile faded and he started ahead.

'My name is Miss Sophie Dove,' she offered, as way of introduction.

'I know,' he said.

'How?'

He gave her back her letter.

'Oh, of course. So who are you?'

As if he had not heard her he crossed the busy street, making sure she was by his side and walked across the veranda of a hotel. It seemed as if it belonged to a different time and place. Once inside she could have imagined herself back in England, only there she would have remained on the outside of such a building looking in. Here with her annoying, yet handsome, stranger she was being escorted into the reception area and people were welcoming them as if they belonged there.

# 3

'Mr Wells, welcome, welcome.' A man in a very smart day suit walked over to where they stood.

Her stranger looked at him and removed his hat. For the first time she saw that his shoulder length hair was as dark in the light as it was with the shadow that the brim cast over it. He ran a hand through it before offering to shake the man's hand.

'Giles,' he said in greeting.

'How goes life on the old plantation?' There was a smirk on the suited man's face. 'Still not tempted by the attractions of Sydney, eh?' He glanced at Sophie, 'Or are we?'

The pleasant smile on Mr Wells' face set into a line. 'Wrong on all accounts Giles, I take it business is good.' He moved the man away from Sophie toward the counter of the hotel reception. Sophie and her bag were left by a desk where a man sat shuffling papers and writing numbers. He glanced up at her coolly, nodded, and then returned to his business. She wondered if she was supposed to stay there or go with her stranger — Mr Wells. One gesture of his fingers from across the foyer told her she was expected to wait.

The hotel door was opened and parcels were brought in. Two lads carrying the carefully wrapped goods approached the desk where the man worked with his papers. They looked ill at ease and she had to smile at them as they nervously approached the clerk at the desk.

'Deliveries for Mr Wells, mister,' one said quietly.

The man looked up, placing his quill carefully back upon its rest. He checked the number of parcels methodically against a piece of paper then, in his own time, looked at the elder lad who was struggling to bear his burden. 'Set them down there . . . carefully.' He pointed to the floor next to where Sophie was standing. Charming, she thought, I am to be left with the baggage.

The anxious lads placed the parcels on the floor next to Sophie's bag. The man raised an eyebrow at her as if she were in the way. The lads left quickly, the elder lingering by the doorway just long enough to admire the fine two storey building — so different and out of place considering its surroundings.

'Miss, we do not usually have single females loitering in our reception area. It hardly looks good for our hotel, now does it?' He gestured to a porter who came over instantly. 'Take these parcels to Mr Wells' room, twenty-three, and lock the door after you.' He held out a key with a card attached bearing the number of the room, ignoring Sophie's flushed cheeks and indignation at his offered insult.

'I am a good friend of Mr Wells!' she snapped.

'I should imagine you are,' he

muttered as he sat back down.

Sophie walked to where she had seen Mr Wells take the man he called Giles. They were sitting in a lounge area. She walked to the archway which separated this from the open area of the reception. Sophie felt out of place, but it was a far safer place to be than walking around the streets of the harbour. She put her head up, shoulders back and decided she would join her 'friend'. She was missing something . . . Her bag! Turning to retrieve it, because it possessed her only belongings she had to face life in this foreign land. She had nothing else save what she stood up in and all that she carried, so she quickly returned to the place by the desk, grateful that the obnoxious man was busy talking to a man by the door. The bag had gone. Seeing the porter who had taken Mr Wells' parcels up to his room returning along a corridor, she stopped him. 'Excuse me, there was a bag here,' she began to explain.

'Yes, miss. I put it with the rest of Mr Wells' things,' he explained. The key to the room was still in his hand.

'Good,' she smiled at him, thinking fate was leading her a different way. 'Please show me where it is as I need to refresh before joining Mr Wells for dinner.' She held her head high, copying the way of this class of people whom she had studied but never been a part of. Servants were not asked to do things, they were told what to do. Sophie was pleasant in manner but firm as though she had no doubt he would follow her order.'

His hesitation was only momentary whilst he glanced at the man from behind the desk who was still in animated discussion.

'This way miss,' he offered.

Sophie followed him down a corridor. They passed five doors, turned up a flight of stairs and then followed another corridor to a room at the end, marked '23'. He unlocked it and she stepped inside.

'Could you arrange for some warm water to be brought up as I need to wash, please and a plate of mutton and damper?' She smiled at him.

'Certainly, miss . . . anything else?' There was almost a hint of sarcasm there.

'A warm drink — coffee or tea perhaps.'

'I will see what we can do, miss.' He hesitated. Sophie swallowed. Was she supposed to give him some money? Her resolve, her ignorance, her bluff was rapidly running out. 'Was there something?' she asked.

'Miss . . . ' he paused, 'No matter, I'll have the food and water sent up.'

'Please,' Sophie stopped him, curious to know what he was to say, 'Tell me?'

'You are fresh off a boat. You don't know this world yet. Take care. Never leave anything you value where it can be taken. Least of all yourself.'

She looked at him, curiously. 'You saw me disembark?' She asked, realising that this was a small town still really, or at least the harbour was. Ships from England did not arrive every day.

'No, I'm too busy to go gawking. You look happy and healthy, miss. Just take care you stay that way.' He winked at her and left, taking the key with him.

Sophie closed the door. The bed took centre of the room, the boarded floor only displaying one rug at the side of the bed. Sophie went to the window opposite; here a table and a high backed chair were positioned. The wharf was a hive of activity and in the distance she could see the square rigs of the barque. Her eyes dropped down to the street below. Convicts, soldiers, men, women . . . whores. A carriage caught her eyes as she saw a bonnet she recognised. Mercy was with a soldier of rank being taken away in the fine vehicle. It stood out from the ox and carts, drays and wagons which trundled back and fore. So, thought Sophie, she had found a way out of this mess. Sophie could only see the back of the bonnet so she could not see the face, to read if it was a solution that pleased the woman or not. She turned back to the room. Her bag was stacked against the far wall next to the parcels and a leather case, which she took to belong to Mr Wells. It was made from fine leather, strong like its owner, and compact. He only carried the minimum he needed, she mused. No excess baggage for him.

There was a knock on the door which made her jump.

'Yes,' she said anxiously, her voice not as confident as it had been.

'Water miss,' the female voice replied.

She opened the door. Two servants entered. One place a hot jug of water on the table near the window with towel, soap and bowl. The other brought food on a plate and a tankard which was placed on the seat of the chair, there being no space left on the table. The two servants dipped a quick curtsey and left closing the door behind them.

Without a moment to stop and consider further she picked up the plate and tankard, sat herself on the edge of the bed and ate. She had forgotten how long it had been since she had taken any victuals until the smell and warmth permeated the air of the food entering the room. Once sated, she placed the clean plate and empty tankard on the floor outside the door, so she would not be disturbed and quickly set to, washing herself. Having no idea what she would do next or how she would explain her actions to Mr Wells, she decided to make the most of her lot whilst she was able to. Removing her dress and feeling the warmth of the cloth as she moved the soapy cloth over her arms, lifting her chemise and stoking the warm moist fabric over her body. Her skin felt instantly refreshed as the stale smell of sweat was replaced by the fragrant odour of the soap. She looked to the door and hearing no noise outside of approaching feet she released her pantaloons and completed her wash. In her bag she had one other set of undergarments, basic, fresh and clean.

She wasted no time in unpacking them and letting the fresh linen fabric fall over her freshly washed skin.

'Heaven', she whispered.

* * *

Matthias Wells eventually finished his business with Giles, a necessary evil as he owned a vast warehouse that Matt used for his supplies. They understood one another which suited Wells fine. He realised that time had slipped and thought about the girl waiting in the lobby. He knew she would be hungry, but perhaps she had now become someone else's problem. Many affluent men would have passed by her, she was not so naive as to realise she would need the patronage of a man to survive here. Not him, though. He had no interest in being taken for a fool again. His heart would stay detached from any woman he met, other parts of him he would be more generous with, but not with a naive, hopeful wench dreaming of her ideal future. This country created dreamers and then smashed them. Matthias was not for smashing — not anymore.

He was relieved when there was no trace of the wench. So it had not taken her long to find a ticket to a different world. Good. One problem he had no need of had just been solved.

'My packets, Jenson, did they arrive?' he asked the man behind the desk, who promptly stood up

'Yes, Mr Wells, all stacked neatly in your room.'

'Good,' Matthias answered, without stopping.

'Under the care I understand of your 'friend'', the man added.

Matthias paused, staring back at the man, who was obviously surprised by the cold dark look which had penetrated Matthias eyes.

'Explain!' he snapped.

'Your lady friend. She is . . . ' he lowered his voice, 'making herself ready, sir.' He cleared his throat. 'We

42

had the water and food sent in as she requested.'

'Did you, indeed!'

He walked on. So much for the meal ticket he thought she had found. However, if she thought he was such a fool then she had another new 'experience' coming. He had offered her a helping hand, a way for her to find a husband or man to look after the little fool, and she was latching her hooks into him. He took the stairs two at a time.

No one moved in on his territory, whether it be a rented room, or his land. He looked along the corridor and as if stalking a wild animal silently moved toward the door. If he found her with her thieving hands in his belongings she would rue the day she ever took Matthias Thaddeus Wells for a milksop. He placed his hand on the door handle and opened it, flinging it wide.

# 4

Standing in the doorway, his tall frame almost filling the width of the open space, he had envisioned seeing the harpy sprawled invitingly on his bed having already rifled his belongings and assessed his worth. What greeted his eyes was not what he expected.

He entered the room, the atmosphere humid. Matthias had looked forward to washing the dust and sweat from his body and then to take his time to assess his purchases, finding peace somewhere in his troubled soul, whilst preparing it for the return, ready to face his future alone. In this room he had sought to know no one else's problems, and just come to terms with his own, to mind his own business. Matthias let the door close slowly behind him, placed his rifle against the wall, and tossed his hat onto the bed — the empty bed. He walked over to the table and chair, having made sure that the fine hair he had placed across the clasp of his bag had not been disturbed. So she was a lost soul, but no thief.

Sophie was curled up in the chair, looking clean and fresh-faced in her white chemise and pantaloons, made of simple linen. She was hugging her dress to her and was sound asleep. Her hair had been washed and brushed through with a worn out comb. He picked it up looking at the gaps where its teeth were missing. His tortoiseshell one, with the silver backbone inlaid lay untouched by her hand.

She was leaning awkwardly against the hard back of the chair in a foetal position, clutching the coarse dress to her almost naked body. It was too heavy a cloth to wear in such a climate at this time of year. He looked at the hem which had been skilfully patched where the fabric had threaded on the edge.

Picking up her bag he found that it was light, not even half full. Looking inside, he saw she had another slightly better cotton dress which had once been a pretty cobalt blue. It would no doubt bring out the colour of her eyes. He smiled to himself, realising for the first time that he had noted them, also the spark of life that had burned deep within them. When all around her was falling apart, her future plans destroyed, she had not cried, pleaded or thrown herself on the mercy of the law when she realised she had been duped.

Her discarded undergarments had been rolled neatly and placed in the bottom of the bag; even that appeared to have been well used. Other than a nightshirt, two pairs of worn stockings and a few coins in a purse, the girl had nothing. She certainly lacked any item which had been purchased as new for her, that was certain. There were no trinkets, tokens of home, no keepsake — nothing. How unlike Beatrice she was. Yet she had not presumed to use his things or taken what was not hers, other than making use of the room and eaten a plate of food which he would no doubt have to pay for. In this new land he could have her arrested as a thief, just like he could have in the old land for taking such liberties. Or he could use her if he decided to take her to 'market' — the hidden one which would trade on victims such as Sophie. Why had the little fool placed her trust in him?

Matthias heard the tray being removed from outside the room and quickly took the balled up garments from her bag, opening the door quickly. The maid jumped back.

'If you can have these laundered and cleaned by morning there will be a coin in it for you,' he said, and tossed the small bundle to her.

She tucked them under her arm and nodded, smiling knowingly at him. Matthias returned to the room. He cared not what people thought was happening inside it, his life was his own.

Looking at the young woman in the

chair he wondered why she should have chosen to latch onto him. She could have cornered an officer; she was young, pretty, and had shown a spark of spirit. He was not soft. Carving a home out of this wild, hungry and treacherous land had proved that. Eight years ago he had been her age, landing here for the first time, his heart and head filled with thoughts of adventure, full of ideas and self importance. He glanced in the looking glass. The tanned skin, creased by the eyes told of eight hard years of forging a future. Nearly thirty, he thought, still single and no nearer his dream now than then despite his wealth.

He looked at Sophie's form curled awkwardly upon the chair and smirked. If they had met then he would not have been so tolerant with her, for then a fire had raged in him also, an angry one, yet now it was all but sated and had almost died out. Beatrice had gone. He had beaten the land, bushrangers, challenged the law and almost died from a snake bite, yet a woman had nearly broken him. Where was the raging fire he had once?

He slid his arms under her. The dress fell to the floor as he scooped her carefully up and lifted her onto the bed. Matthias felt her warmth through the thin fabric and breathed in her freshness. Placing her carefully down on the bed cover, she stretched out responding to the softness underneath her body, and then curled up again, not wanting to stir.

He smiled as he watched her movements. Lovely, he thought. Reaching out he took the top cover and draped it over her slim frame, his hand lingering to softly stroke the contour of her side. She did not stir, but muttered something inaudible. The journey, he knew had caught up with her. He admired the curves of her body. Her firm breasts straining against the chemise as she rolled over unwittingly inviting. He turned away.

Walking over to the window he stared

down. Was Matthias Thaddeus Wells a changed man? Was he about to do something kind? Glancing back at the prone figure on the bed he had a yearning to do something other than act as a 'gentleman' should as his father would have said. He felt more like doing what a 'gentleman would' to such a vulnerable wench. An image of Beatrice returned, churning his gut as she always had, at one time with desire and longing, now with hatred and loathing, mainly of himself, for her face still haunted him. He told himself he did not need a woman, not now. He would not share his home with one again. He would hire or pay for what he needed. A wife — a woman, was not necessary.

Matthias collected his hat, picked up his rifle and locked the door as he left. He was no saint, but this country had destroyed so many lives, why toss another young wench at it. The rest of her group had been dissolved into the inns or soldiers' beds, within the year those that fared well and survived bagging themselves an officer, would be Beatrice's in the making. The country already had one too many. So, he asked himself wisely, why not help this one?

Why not indeed, his internal voice replied. For want of nothing better to do at the moment, Matthias Thaddeus Wells decided to be kind.

When Sophie woke, the room was in pitch darkness. She realised she must have slept soundly for hours. Sophie reached out under the coverlet, feeling the sheet, sensing warmth that was not from her own body. She also realised she was in the bed in her undergarments without even her nightdress on. How had she got there? She only remembered resting her head on her dress whilst she sat in the chair. Sophie had only thought to rest a few moments as the feeling of tiredness had hit her quite suddenly, as if everything had drawn to a halt: her journey, the swaying, her plans and, temporarily, her future. She had been overwhelmed by life and had needed rest. Then, in the darkness she had heard something and knew it was not her own breath which she was listening to. She slowly extended her arm until it touched someone warm lying next to her.

He was in the bed with her. Her fingers touched the flesh of his naked back. She stood up quickly making sure she was still fastened and felt normal, not knowing what in fact she was expecting to find, for surely her sleep could not have been that deep. Her eyes adjusted to the gloom as she looked around the floor by the chair, feeling for her dress.

'Lost something?' his sleepy voice asked.

'I fell asleep . . . I . . . ' she began to explain, a feeling of panic growing in her stomach as her dress was nowhere to be found.

'I know, you snored,' he said drily.

'I do not snore!' she said, placing her hands on her hips as if to emphasise her words, then realising as she did she was

52

exposing not only her undergarments, but her body also.

He smiled at her, looking at her appreciatively from under heavy lids. Casually he raised himself up until he was sitting on the bed. His chest was firm, but as she lit a lamp on the table she saw that he had a three inch scar across his collarbone to the right of his neck. He pulled himself up the bed until his back was resting against the wooden bed head and casually drew the sheet up to his waist, still watching her. There was no fat to be seen on his broad chest just firm muscle. His strong arms were casually resting upon his drawn up knees.

'No, you don't snore, that at least is true. Get back in, woman.' He patted the mattress next to him.

'I won't . . . I can't. You don't understand what has happened here. It was not my intention to stay. I just wanted to . . . ' Sophie could see the humour in his eyes even though his face was held in a sombre expression.

53

'You intended to use my room, eat my food and leave without paying your way. Is that what you meant to do, Sophie?' He raised an eyebrow.

'No! Not like that. I just wanted to wash. They brought my bag to this room with your things. It was an accident, sir.' She was looking around for her dress in her state of undress, shamefully aware that she had acted badly and that he seemed to be enjoying her discomfort.

'So where were you going to go?' He waited a moment but she did not answer.

'Where is my dress?' Sophie had checked her bag. There was no underwear in it and only her best dress.

'Answer the question.'

She looked at him and stared defiantly back at his dark eyes. Eyes that were difficult to read, offering depth and determination, but she believed in her instincts and they told her that he did not wish to harm her, despite her foolhardiness. 'To find employment,' she answered.

'Mercy has left to keep a captain company in his home. Thea has agreed to marry a lieutenant. She will at least be considered respectable until, of course, he leaves for home. He is not duty bound to take her with him. Matilda has left with a gold prospector and the others are finding matches of one kind or another along with less fortunate women who came off the boat brought for the purpose of . . . Once the dealing is done, they too will have homes of a sort. So where would Sophie go and with whom?' He tilted his head on one side and watched her standing there, arms folded, uneasy and ill at ease, but defiant.

'What of Mr Simmons?' she asked, not wanting to admit that she was completely lost in this new world. 'This is of his making. We trusted him.'

'He is keeping the soldiers company as he serves his first night in the cells for his part in corrupting the lives of young women. Not, of course, that they will do anything to help the plight of the young women. Justice must still be seen to be done and they benefit from the spoils.'

He was looking at her with his fringe hanging slightly over his eyes. She noted the heavy sarcasm in his voice.

'I don't know where I could seek employment. I don't even know where my dress is.' She stepped to the foot of the bed. 'Help me, please? Don't ask me to join them or entertain you for that matter. I can cook, sew, I am used to animals, I follow orders well and work hard. Let me work for you — honestly, and I will be a loyal servant. You are a man who does not need to bully or take the likes of me. Help me to find a decent position in a decent home and please tell me what you did with my other undergarments and the dress?' She stopped talking when he laughed at her, and shook his head.

He flicked half of the bedding back. 'Blow out the lamp, you will not find your dress. I took it and gave it to those less fortunate than you. Your underthings will be returned laundered tomorrow. I have a long journey to make and I need rest. I will take you away from here and we shall see where your path leads, but for now be quiet, cover yourself before my resolve weakens, and sleep. Tomorrow is another day, Sophie and then we shall talk. For now, sleep in a warm bed because, for the next seven nights you shall not have one.'

'You did what to my dress?' Sophie blew out the lamp and climbed in, placing a pillow between them.

'You heard.'

'I only have one other, you know it. You have been in my bag. I have little enough. Could you not have left that with me?' She was appalled that she had one dress left to her. What if she ripped it? What would she wear if it needed to be cleaned as surely it would in this climate?

'Trust me, or leave me, but be quiet.'

57

Sophie lay near the edge of the bed, listening. His breathing became heavier. He made no effort to touch her and so she slept until the sun shone in. Activity outside brought strange noises into the room and she stirred. Feeling relaxed despite having such a weight on her mind, she realised there was another weight — on her stomach. Her hand slipped down over Matthias'. He was sprawled over the pillow, still sleeping but as he felt her touch he began to move his fingers, gently massaging her stomach. She was about to try and lift him off her, ignoring the pleasant feelings it stimulated within her when he woke. Heavy lids opened slowly. Sophie lay there looking at his face as he slowly smiled, his hand slipping slightly higher as she moved it away. The feel of his warmth as his finger moved across her chemise sent strange feelings running through her limbs. He lifted his head and kissed her lips quickly before she slipped out of bed.

'Good morning, rabbit,' he said as he

stood up at his side and stretched. As he rose she saw the scars on his back before he pulled his shirt over his head. She looked at him, unaware that she was being silhouetted by the sunlight from the window.

'You are a flogged man, sir,' she said quietly.

'And you are a beautiful woman,' he replied, staring at her body, apparently not caring that she knew this about him . . .

Sophie grabbed the sheet off the bed and wrapped it around her body. She bent to her bag to pull out her good dress.

'Not that, these.' He tossed a bundle to her.

She looked at it pulling the garments loose. 'These are breeches . . . shirt . . . and . . . ' she looked at him in surprise. 'You would have me dress as a man?'

'I would have you dress as a man, yes, for your own comfort and safety, Sophie. If anyone sees us from afar you will be as a younger brother and not as my woman.'

She looked at him indignantly.

'Or wife. Few would care over the difference here.' He pulled on his boots and tossed her a hat and jacket like his own coat.

'I have not the coin to pay for these, Mr Wells.' Sophie swallowed, feelings of guilt starting to bother her as she had already eaten the man's food.

'Did I ask for money?' He was fastening his belt buckle.

'No, but I should not be indebted; it is not right,' Sophie answered, and even she thought her words sounded pathetic under the circumstances.

'Nothing which has happened to you in the last twenty-four hours has been right, has it?' He walked over to her. 'Has it?'

'No,' she agreed.

'I doubt that there has been much about your life to date which could be morally attributed to the word fair.'

'I don't want your pity, sir,' she

answered as she stood holding the strange, yet precious garments to her. They were new. They were a gift and she had not owned such things before. Her grip tightened on them.

'Good, for I shall not give it. What happened to 'Mr Wells' for I do not wish you to address me as 'sir' — or 'master'.' He leaned towards her.

'Good, for no one will be my master,' she answered sharply, his lips only inches away from her he stared into her eyes as if delving and tormenting her soul. She stood still, playing out this game of bluff.

'Get dressed,' he said, and planted a kiss on her lips before she could dodge away. Satisfied he had played his game out, he placed his hat on his head and walked to the door. 'Stay here. I will make sure my wagon and supplies are safe, then I shall return with food and we shall then be on our way. Run if you want to, rabbit, but I shall not linger to find you. The choice is yours.'

# 5

The wagon, Mr Wells had told her, was going to be loaded and would be waiting for them outside the hotel. Then they were starting out on a journey to who knew where — she didn't, and shamefully, perhaps, she did not care. So long as she was not doomed into a forced marriage of convenience or worse. Whatever wrong Wells had committed to get a flogging, she was sure it was not justified, as he was a gentleman in the true meaning of the word. He had proved that to her, hadn't he? She glanced at the newly made bed and could not help her cheeks flush slightly at the thought of his touch.

Sophie had never felt as strange as this before, she was free in a way she had never known before and now she was even wearing a man's attire. She was experiencing a way of moving unrestricted by the heavy skirt of her dress, and she liked it. Everything fitted — sort of. The breeches did and the boots. The shirt was baggy and loose and the coat hung over it when she put it on so no contour of her form could be seen. It was longer than it should be or she was shorter, but it would do. The final piece of her new persona was the hat. The wide brim certainly would cast a shadow over her face. Again it was slightly lower on her brow than it should ideally be, but her hair helped to pad it out. She played with her hair, putting it up, and then letting it down. Then after brushing it so she could tie it back, which she then slipped under her coat collar, she decided that this was the best option.

She walked over to the window, her back to the door. She heard the knock and ignored it thinking it was someone wanting Mr Wells, so she thought she had best remain silent. It opened and a maid walked in carrying her laundered garments. The girl let out a gasp as she saw the figure by the window.

'Sorry, sir, I thought you were out. Here are the lady's undergarments.'

Sophie's eyes widened, but she kept her head turned away, looking out of the window. She raised a gloved hand in a dismissive gesture, clearing her throat with as deeper note as she could muster, as if she had begun to say something, but it had stuck in her gullet.

'Would that be all, sir?' the lass asked.

Sophie nodded, whilst coughing and still looking away. The girl left.

Sophie smiled and looked at her clean and pressed linen garments. Carefully, she placed them inside her bag. Her old dress had also been returned. So he had not given it away. She smiled; Mr Matthias Wells was a tease. She returned to her vigil as she had seen Mr Wells walking into a store further along the street. It seemed so strange to her that she had been with this man such a short while yet in that time her life had changed completely. She had even shared a bed with him. She would have been turned out as an immoral woman for that at the workhouse, left destitute, her fate sealed.

She watched below, seeing her new friend come out of the shop carrying another parcel. He was clearly stocking up for a long journey or a time away from the city. She could not imagine how remote his land might be, yet, she seemed strangely attracted to the idea of seeing it. How many nights had he said it would take in the open? Eight. How appealing that thought was to her; to lie under the stars, at one with nature. She refused to think about the stories of snakes and serpents, reptiles that bite and insects that could kill a man. Sophie was about to turn away from the window when she saw a familiar figure following behind Mr Wells. It was the sailor who had approached her at the dockside, and that Matthias had pulled the rifle on in the docks. He looked as if he was following him, but at a distance so that Matthias could not see the shadow he had unwittingly acquired. Sophie left the room, picking up the rifle as she went and slinging it across her back as she had seen Matthias do.

With her hat upon her head and with as bold and manly a stride as she could muster she strode down the corridor, stairs and across the foyer and out into the street. Taking only a moment to get her bearings, she saw the sailor nipping down an alleyway towards what appeared to be a stable yard, and guessed that was where Matthias had been heading. She crossed the main road, not looking at passing soldiers or tradesmen, keeping her head slightly lowered and her gaze fixed firmly in the direction she was heading, in the path of the brute who had tried to intimidate her when she had arrived such as short time ago. Soon she too had disappeared down the narrow street between two buildings.

She swung the rifle to her front and held it in her hands as if born to it. On the farm, she had used one to pot hares, taught by the owner's son who had come back from the wars restless and ill at ease, with little interest in farming, but with a love of this new firearm. She had learned to use it with some skill, not as he, but enough to kill a hare. Here, she only wanted to frighten the man off, if he was about to cause her new friend problems.

She could not see either of them, so she leaned against the side of the building and listened.

★ ★ ★

Matthias was pleased to be leaving. The wagon was being loaded and would be guarded until he returned with his horse. The wench, he would find a home for, but not here. On the parameters of the city there were outlying farms. Perhaps, there, he would be able to leave her. Realising his decision to take the woman with him was rash, he was rethinking his options. But then, why had he enjoyed buying her such clothes to travel in if he was to desert her here in Sydney? Parramatta would have more choice; fewer women of any repute had made it that far. The female factory was full of the unfortunates. Sophie was new to the land. At home she may have been frowned upon for her poverty, but here she would be valued as young, strong and healthy — and a maid. She would find a husband or position there. Then he could travel on to his own land.

For some reason, his enthusiasm waned. It was no good. He had to return, Beatrice would have gone. His land would still be there. A land he once craved and loved. If he returned and his home was no longer any joy to him, then he would come this way again, but to sell it. What then?

He had no answer, but then he heard a question.

'Where's your rifle now, boy?'

He turned slowly, recognising the sailor who had tried his luck with Sophie.

'Haven't you seen enough of it already?' he asked, silently cursing his stupidity for leaving it in the room with Sophie. His head was not thinking straight. Being caught like a greenhorn in an alleyway was stupid, and Matthias knew he was not that — although Beatrice had fooled him.

'Now, there is just you and me here and a nag in there. You must have earned a coin or two from the wench. I want my share of it, or of her, but before I take it, I want to see your face in the dirt where it belongs.' He balled his fist. 'You're an ex navy man. I can smell your kind from ten yards off. Worse than a rotten fish is the smell of a half-baked officer.'

He came forward. Matthias bent to put down his parcel and then as the man rushed him, which was what he expected the coward to do, he swung up with two tightly woven fists into the man's gut. It was hard and his blow left little impression on the man's stomach. He had a gut, but underneath he had well-used muscle hard as mahogany. It was then Matthias knew he was in trouble. The thwack of the man's fist against his shoulder, merely confirmed it.

Matthias sprang up, knowing a second blow would catch him before he could strike again, but instead there was a cracking sound and the man crumpled. As he fell forward, Matthias rolled over and saw Sophie standing holding the barrel of his precious rifle, having used it like a club to strike down his mugger.

'Have you no respect?' he snapped, and grabbed the weapon, checking it for damage. The man moaned, but did not move. Both ignored him.

'I just saved your life!' Sophie responded, as a parcel was thrust into her arms.

'Hold this, and do not exaggerate,' he said, having satisfied himself that the weapon was undamaged, before disappearing into the stables to reappear with his horse. He then man-handled the sailor over the rump of the animal and climbed into the saddle. 'Go to the hotel. Wait near the wagon. We will leave as soon as I return.'

'Where will you go with him? What are you going to do with the man?' Sophie asked, not sure what he intended.

'Return him to where he belongs — the sea,' he replied coolly.

Her eyes widened. Her mouth hung open.

'I will return him to the ship where he can serve the rest of the time here in the galley. He will not pester us or anyone else anymore!' His manner was sharp. He had been caught unawares, his skin saved by a female and to top it all that same female obviously did not doubt he was capable of tossing the man to the fishes. Matthias wondered if any woman was capable of seeing well in him. Was this one as fickle as . . . ?

Bea . . . He did not want to even think her name. From now on it was a word banned from his mind and his lips. Like Sophie would be if she did not show more trust. He rode off, knowing full well he had been embarrassed by his stupidity and the fact that he had broken a personal promise — never to be indebted to a female again. This female was young, beautiful and sincere, but that was not what this land respected. It would soon harden and break her like many who had come here to live out their dream only to find themselves living through a nightmare soon.

As Matthias rode toward the ship where he turned the sailor over to their own justice, he wondered again if he had been stupid to become involved in Sophie's life. He doubted the wisdom of his rash decision until he rode up to the wagon, on which was sat what to all would look at first glance like a young man. Something within him stirred. Something which made him doubt his wisdom, yet touched his very soul. He had been bored with life. He had been worn down by disappointment, yet something in her eyes, that sparkle of life and optimism had touched the dying flame of anticipation within his soul. For better or worse, she would share his next journey as far as Parramatta, and then he would decide if she should accompany him home.

# 6

They rode out of Sydney with a full wagon. He took the reins and Sophie sat quietly by his side. His horse was tied to the back of the wagon following behind.

'Once we leave this place behind us I shall ride on and you shall take over the wagon. Can you do that?' He looked down but could only see the top of her hat.

Sophie did not want to look up at him although she sensed his eyes were seeking hers. He had given her such an expression of what she presumed was hatred when she had questioned his intentions over the injured sailor. Although she had every reason to loathe the man for being a brute and a coward, she had thought the worst of Mr Wells and, in doing so, had placed him in the same category of ruffian as

74

the sailor. Unfortunately, her reaction had been so quick that her doubts had shown, and in that moment she had lost his respect.

She nodded her understanding as she had no doubt he was not seeking her agreement. She sat straight as her hat was suddenly flipped off the back of her head. Sophie's head shot up and her eyes met his, challenging his rash action.

Sophie grabbed her hat before it rolled along the back of the wagon and risked falling onto the black dust of the road. 'There was no need for that, was there?' she asked, and muttered, 'Childish,' as she placed it back on her head.

'Then answer me properly. It is you who is like a child!' he replied.

Sophie noted there was that lighter note in his voice again and not the anger which had filled his tone in the town. Reluctantly she answered him, 'Yes, that would be fine with me. I used the cart on the farm.'

'Good was there anything you did

not do on the farm?'

'Of course there was. But I think if you want you can learn a lot from opportunities. You just have to make the most of what God throws at you.' She resumed her quiet, thoughtful, demeanour as the wagon steadily moved through the outskirts of the settlement.

'Well then. You are quite a philosopher. Why so quiet?' he asked her.

'I owe you an apology, sir.' Sophie decided that, if this was to be a long journey, they had better start out on the right side of each other's personality.

'You do?' His voice withheld a note of surprise. 'For abusing my rifle in such a dangerous and thoughtless way?'

'No, for doubting you. For thinking you were capable of killing a man in cold blood. I am sorry for that. I didn't think it through back there. I should have known that you would take him to the ship and have him clapped in irons or whatever the term is.' She glanced up at him and saw that he was half smiling at her.

'Why should you know that? You have no way of knowing if I would kill a man or not. How is it that you have decided to trust me, Sophie?' He was watching the road as it found its way out of Sydney in the direction of the Blue Mountains. 'You know so little of me. I could have fed the fishes with that man and no one would have known, so how can you be so certain that I would not?' He was holding the reins carefully in his gloved hands, but his attention was fully upon her.

'Instinct,' she said honestly, and was rewarded with an open laugh. His head tilted back. Although he seemed to be mocking her reasoning, Sophie saw the youth in his face, the laughter lines, and a light in his eyes which shone as if he had not laughed so hard for a very long time — too long she guessed. He was a man who had started to age through sobriety; she wanted to teach him to laugh more often, for it suited him.

'You risk your life and reputation on a mere instinct. Is this the same reliable intuition that led you to an office with a man who promised you a better life in a strange new land?'

'Yes,' she answered simply.

'You trust it still?' he asked, the smile subsiding as curiosity took its place.

'Yes, because I have not found it wanting yet; I came here for a new start — a chance to be something I could never be at home, and look at me,' she replied, and opened her arms as if showing the change in her situation with joy.

'Sophie, you could so easily have had the chance to become something you were not at home had I not been there at the time.' He raised a brow.

'True, but you were, so I trust it still,' she smiled confidently at him.

'How simple your thinking is — yet you are not a simple fool.'

Sophie laughed; a dimple appeared upon her cheek as she thought what a marvellous insulting compliment his words reluctantly formed.

'You do not fear where I will take

you, Sophie? Have you not considered who else could be there waiting? Would you risk your life again on a whim or a fancy? This is a harsh country, Sophie. It is not one you can trifle with and run from when things go badly, back home to your mama's hearth. This is one that will take your life, if you make one simple mistake. You . . . '

Her head went down, the hat acting once more as a barrier between him, and her eyes welled up instantly, filled with sadness at the impossible statement made within his words.

He stopped talking, slowed the wagon to a stop. Resting the reins in his hands, he toyed with them for a moment before addressing her directly. With no smile, no grin and no humour he placed a dusty gloved finger beneath her chin and turned her face to meet his. 'Now, it is I who owe you an apology. That was unkind. You said you have never known your mama and for that comment I am truly sorry. I did know mine and I sorely miss her still.'

'Apology accepted,' she replied awkwardly. 'Should we continue the journey and you can tell me honestly if you have decided to be rid of me so soon?' She looked boldly at Matthias, realising she had a way of wrong-footing him; she did not react as he expected her to. It was as if he thought women were predictable and she was not. It was a feeling she liked.

He tilted his hat back slightly so that she could see his dark features clearly. 'Lady, when I decide that time is here, you will have no need to ask me that question, it will be quite clear.' His manner was firm, voice giving controlled depth, and manner stern. 'I shall give you a word of advice before others you might meet do. I am capable of much more than your innocent mind has assumed. Be wary of me, Miss Dove, for I am a man who is not so easily read as you think.'

Sophie smiled, 'Good, then our journey will be interesting and we shall not misunderstand each other then.'

He shook his head, handed her the reins and climbed onto his own horse. 'Keep at a steady pace, don't lose concentration and watch out for ruts.'

Without further word he rode ahead as they left the township behind and headed towards the mountains.

* * *

Matthias wanted to check the road ahead. It was a rough country and, once settlements were left behind, the journey became even more perilous. Not just from the local animals, reptiles and insects, but from bushrangers, escaped convicts; desperate men and women failing to make an honest living in this land of empty promises turning to whatever means they could find in order to live.

He wanted to ride on his own. Sophie was an enigma, innocent yet worldly. He wanted to protect her and at the same time teach her some life lessons. She deserved both.

# 7

Matthias was absent for a few hours. Sophie kept the wagon moving at a steady pace, singing to herself any and every tune she knew; from sea shanties, hymns to folk songs. The trees, strange old eucalyptus trees were filled with budgerigars — fascinating and beautiful as they flew up into the sky, disturbed by her presence. Occasionally a cockatoo shrieked; the creatures, the sounds, were so different to the farm. Sophie was fascinated by everything, it was as if she had arrived in a new land and discovered a whole new world, as if God had created every country so that his children should all sample something different. It was a notion she found appealing. Life here was so colourful compared to the sparse cold walls of the workhouse she was raised in. Here there was space, variety, adventure and Matthias Wells; she knew she was falling in love with it all.

'Do you always sing?' His voice did not surprise her for she had sensed he was circling around her through the woodland. She had heard the horse in the distance and decided that it must be Matthias' because it had not frightened her. She had once been followed by a man when she worked on the farm; she had sensed the danger as he sighted her as his prey and had managed to out run him. Besides, she had seen that Mattias kept a large knife under the seat; if she needed to she would fight man or beast.

'When I am passing time, yes,' she glanced back at him, 'Don't you?'

He ignored her question. 'You are dressed as a youth, but you sound like a woman, a young woman. It rather undermines the disguise, does it not?' He rode alongside and slipped from the saddle to the wagon, tethering his horse's reins to the side; it reluctantly fell into place behind. He then steered the wagon away from the track to a clearing near the banks of a broad river. Slowing the wagon until it came to a stop, he positioned it carefully so that it was clear of the trees but away from the actual bank, and shielded from the road. Once he was satisfied that it was secured, he saw to the comfort of his horse and unhitched the animal from the wagon. Matthias then set to feeding them, seeing to their water and finally setting a fire going on the land between the wagon and the river.

He said nothing. Sophie watched, fascinated. He acted as though he had done this many times before. No creature surprised him; he dispatched a snake and stamped on a large spider before tossing the insect into the fire he had set. He had used the resources that nature provided to build the small fire, taking great care to clear the surrounding area; she presumed that this was in case the dry vegetation was set ablaze. He had a small pot, he used his own dried herbs and some of the plants found in the wild to add to the meat, which he had stripped from the snake. Once all this was simmering away, he then turned to find Sophie, who was seated cross legged on top of a sack on the wagon.

He looked at her as if he had been going to speak, but hesitated for a moment and just stared.

'Will we be staying in an inn tonight, Mr Wells?' Sophie watched the expression change on his face. She found his reactions amusing. He may be worldly, but he had never met a Sophie Dove before. His face showed either surprise because he had been so busy he had forgotten he had a companion, or that she had asked him such a question.

'No inns. No hotels. Just this,' he replied politely and continued to tend the food. When she did not reply, he glanced back at her. 'What are you doing?' he asked.

'Moving things around,' she answered, as she prodded and poked packages to determine where they should go.

'Why?'

'Because, if we are to sleep in the wagon a space will be needed.' Sophie was busy trying to make a gully in the middle by moving sacks, parcels and supplies so that it was possible for them to have some rest in it. 'Do you take first watch and I second, or the other way around, the choice is yours?'

'You sleep underneath it, and I will bed down here by the fire, with one eye open. You sleep. I would not sleep knowing my life was being watched over by someone fresh off the ship who will have never 'watched' before.'

She looked at him, standing tall by the fire, his rifle held in one hand. It was never far from him. When he rode it was slung across his back, when he was busy it was always within his reach. He was, she thought, a man who constantly expected trouble. Was that because of the country or because of his past?

'I don't want to sleep under it. I . . . Can I please sleep in here? I promise I won't open or steal anything.'

She had stopped moving things and was staring straight at him.

He strode over to the side of the wagon. Sophie knelt down to face him from her carefully organised space. 'See, I can sleep here without damaging anything.' She patted the makeshift bed that she had made.

He slung his rifle on his back and leaned onto the side of the vehicle, their faces so close together that she breathed in his musk.

'You are scared.' He stared into her eyes.

'Yes, I am. I have never spent the night outdoors and here every creature is different to those of home. The insects are huge. I would feel safer if I was up here.' Despite admitting a weakness she spoke confidently.

'You sleep here. If it rains you sleep under that rolled up cover with the supplies.'

'Thank you,' she replied quietly, her face so close to his that she decided to kiss his cheek quickly.

He turned his lips to meet hers. Her fleeting kiss lingered as his hand gently cupped the back of her head pulling her to him. What was to have been a natural response, a grateful gesture of thanks at the relief of not having to spend a night awake in fear of being crawled over by insects or bitten by snakes, became an intimate moment. She tried to move her head away but he gently persevered. Her cheeks blushed; her mouth moved with his as desire grew. It was he who pulled away.

He stepped back. She was left there on her knees in the wagon. She steadied herself by holding the side of the vehicle for she felt strange, and inside she was shaking. For once Sophie was lost for words.

He turned his back to her and returned to the cook pot. 'Food's ready,' he announced.

Sophie swallowed. She climbed out of the wagon and walked over to the fire. 'If you are hungry you will eat this and learn to eat whatever fresh food is placed in front of you as we travel. In the inns you are served old meat, poorly cooked with gritty dampers and rum or grog. You'd be lucky to leave with all the possessions you arrived with. Without a man by your side at night you would find others would take his place.' He served her a portion in a can and handed it to her with a spoon.

Sophie nodded and took the can from his hands. She would eat, but she had discovered an appetite which had a growing hunger behind it. It was a hunger that she realised the food would not sate. She spooned her food into her mouth; staring at the flickering flames of the fire she chewed her first ever snake meat in silence.

After the food he showed her how to damp down the fire so that there was no risk of a bush fire taking hold. He showed her where to wash the cans in the river, first checking for animal tracks, and the importance of securing and checking the horses, wagon and goods. The cover was there ready in case of the first downpour of rain. Throughout all his instruction she did not speak, but listened and learned.

'Now you climb into your bed, Sophie, and sleep soundly.'

She hesitated, not knowing if she should say something or not. They had been intimate. She had acted badly and knew he was fully aware that she had responded willingly to his touch. This was a situation in which she did not know what to do.

'Don't tell me the confident Miss Dove does not trust me anymore after one kiss!' he said, as if inviting her to rebel against his mockery. There was a cold undertone in his words that Sophie picked up on, something that told her he had been hurt. She had wrong-footed him again, in some way that she did not understand.

She climbed up onto the wagon and waited for him to turn away before she answered. 'It is not you that I am scared of, Matthias. Goodnight.' She snuggled down in her makeshift bed ignoring the lumps of the sacks around her, and closed her eyes. Tomorrow she would behave better. Tomorrow she would be strong.

★ ★ ★

Matthias stared at the wagon as he settled on the ground. Why had he not scared her? He was capable of it. He wanted to climb in there with her. So what stopped him? His honour? He had lost his faith in that. A flogging and a bitch had destroyed his belief in most things, yet a kiss from a pretty maid and his conscience had been touched. He rolled onto his back and stared at the sky. Tomorrow he would put distance between them. If she thought he was a naive sop that she could hook so easily, she was mistaken.

# 8

The journey to Parramatta continued with both doing their separate jobs, both avoided being close to each other. She took the wagon and he rode on horseback. Conversation when they were together was filled with questions and advice on surviving in this new land. Neither probed the others past and neither talked of their future.

They approached the township. A group of hapless creatures were ahead of them at the side of the road. Two figures who were strewn on the floor appeared to Sophie to be women.

'Are they ill? Do they need help?' she asked and glanced up at Matthias. She was surprised at what she saw. Gone was the gentle relaxed look which she had become used to. Instead, it had been replaced by a cynical expression, which made him look older and hardened to life in a way she had not seen before.

'Keep your head downwards. Wear my gloves and do not speak. We shall pass through this town as soon as we can. We will not be staying here. It is a place where thieves abound; they steal anything they can in order to survive.' His eyes stared ahead. He lowered his hands with the reins and slipped his pistol under the folds of his coat, glancing at the rifle which was placed at his feet.

'Do you think they have a plague here?' she said quietly.

'The plague they have here is one called 'rum' and another called tyranny which has led them to a life bordering anarchy. It is only stopped by a firm rule of law, which has put men in positions of power who created it.' He looked at her. 'No more questions. Do as I say. No matter what I say and what happens, say nothing, look down and do not reveal you are a female.'

'Oh, I remember, this is the place

where I was told I could always find a home and work. It has a factory for females, I suppose like the workhouse. Only I don't wish to ever live in such a place again. Do you know of it? I . . . '

'Silence!' he snapped and Sophie looked down, she was shaken by his reproof but realised she needed to listen more and learn by watching. She supposed there was a time to do without questioning. This was his country not hers. Still she had not been rebuked in such a way since leaving England and the harsh tone in his voice had made her tremble inside, causing her to feel sad, because she had started to trust him. Lost in her thoughts, she was aware of the figures at the side of the wagon.

'Mr, want a shepherd?' an almost toothless man shouted.

'Want company? I am good I am. Can cook, can wash and can whatever you like mister.' A dishevelled woman propped herself against a tree.

'When you can stand straight without

falling over you might find work,' he replied.

'Saucy gent, you is,' she laughed and slid back to the ground. They travelled past. Sophie smiled, but when he tossed the reins to her, stood and turned pointing a pistol at a man who appeared to be standing innocently at the side of the road, she was not laughing anymore.

'Fetch me my parcel back from the shrubbery and place it carefully on the wagon or I will blow what brains you have left out of your ugly head,' Matthias shouted.

'Don't know what you are talkin' about, mister.' He swayed slightly.

'Get it now, or lose a leg.' Matthias placed his thumb on the trigger.

Sophie's hands were trembling. She tried to hold the wagon still. Out of the corner of her eye she noticed another man moving his hand slowly behind his back. He was at the opposite side to Matthias and was therefore out of his vision. Sophie slipped her hand carefully out of the glove and felt for the rifle.

Matthias' finger pulled slowly back on the trigger.

'I only wanted to feed me wife and children. They is starvin' mister. You 'as so much . . . Alright, alright, here . . . ' He bent down to retrieve the stolen parcel.

The other man quickly produced a knife, but before he took one pace forward, Sophie raised the rifle and sited it straight at him. She tried to make her voice sound deep, 'I wouldn't if I were you.'

The man stopped. Whilst she held the gun trained on him, whose face looked as though he wanted to slit her throat, Matthias carefully stepped down, still training the pistol on the man who had retrieved the parcel, who then tossed it into the back of the wagon. Without warning, he struck his would be attacker with the hand holding the pistol. The man folded. Matthias took the knife off him and tossed it onto the wagon. The other man took a run at Matthias, but he turned around and shot, wounding him in the leg. The drunken wench screamed, whilst her man howled in agony.

'You . . . bast . . . ' she did not get time to finish her sentence as two soldiers were riding up the road towards them, swords drawn.

'What happened here?' one asked. Sophie had sat back down steadying the horse and securing the wagon. She tried not to look at the men, concentrating on the horse and feeling frightened as much for Matthias as herself. He had shot a man.

'The blackguard tried to rob me, and this man was about to slit my throat.' He pointed to the man who was trying to regain his senses and stand up. Matthias picked up the knife from the wagon. 'He pulled this out and was trying to run me through.'

One of the soldiers walked his horse over and looked down at the pair of ticket of leave men. They had once been convicts but had earned their freedom so long as they stayed out of trouble. The shot man was still holding his leg. The bullet had done as Matthias had intended, it had cut the flesh winging him, but had not sunk the ball into the leg. By this time, four further soldiers on foot had arrived.

'I know you — Fetcher, isn't it? Ticket of leave. Done it this time you have. Take him!' Two soldiers came forward and dragged the man off with no thought to his wound or the pain.

'I'm innocent! I have a wife and children . . . I' his voice faded away as a fist was raised. He had no stomach for any more pain.

Sophie was aware that the other soldier was mounted on his horse next to the wagon. She could feel his stare, but did not want to look around at him.

'Name?' the soldier with Matthias asked the man whose knife had nearly been the death of him.

'Staple, Benjamin Staple.' His voice was level, calm, and very hard. Sophie could not help but glance towards him. His grizzled face had lines set of stone. Whatever that man had endured in his life had not broken him, but made him a beast beyond humanity. She had seen men broken in the workhouse, women too, through endless toil, reduced rations or solitary confinement. This man's body had endured, but his mind had survived only by switching off the essential traits of his emotions and sensitivity which, to Sophie, made life worth living. She felt a cold fear of him and what he would now be capable of, yet at the same time huge sympathy. Sophie was only too aware that desperation and hunger led people to do things they would never have in more affluent circumstances. It was easy to have morals when your family were well fed, clothed and housed.

'Well, Staple, it will be a flogging at least for you this time, before your fate is determined. No doubt a little journey to Norfolk Island will sort you out. They know how to deal with scum like you.' The soldier laughed, making Sophie swell with disgust.

Staple stood proud. He had obviously recovered his senses. Without warning he suddenly let out a cry of grief, like the howl of an injured wolf. It caused the horse to rear wildly, throwing the soldier to the ground. He landed awkwardly on his head. The group were caught off guard. The other ticket of leave decided to make themselves scarce, the more sober woman helping her drunken friend to walk away propped against her. Matthias had turned back to Sophie. His possessions safe, he seemed to care nothing for the fate of the man. He looked back as the convict ran for his life, sprinting into the bush. The soldiers went after him, with the exception of the other mounted man. He immediately went to his injured friend. Matthias and he, together, lifted the fallen soldier into the back of the wagon. Sophie looked back, and the other soldier saw her.

'Miss, you help him. We need to get him to the barracks.'

She glanced at Matthias and he nodded.

Sophie climbed into the back and tried to make the man as comfortable as she could but thought that the blow to his head, where it had hit a stone, was so severe he may not recover his wits; that is, if he recovered at all.

'I'll go on ahead and have things prepared. Do you know where the barracks are, man?' the soldier asked Matthias as he remounted his horse.

'Yes,' was all Matthias said, as he drove the wagon onwards.

Sophie wondered what was going through his mind. His mood and his appearance had darkened, like his features. She felt uneasy. The soldier knew she was a young woman, dressed as a man, travelling with a settler. Would they treat her with any respect? She shook her head. Her new land, her dream, had just been shadowed by the tinge of a nightmare, as it had when she found herself abandoned on the quayside of this strangely mystifying land.

They passed by a building where the moans and cackles of the inmates could be heard as they drove by.

'Is that the prison, Mr Wells?' she asked.

'That is the Female Factory. It is a cesspit and it would no doubt make your workhouse look like a palace. If a woman is decent when she passes beyond their threshold, she will not be by the first dawn or dusk she spends there. You stay well clear of it.' He did not take his eyes from the road.

'Then the man was threatening me?' she replied, as if shocked that she had not even realised.

'Sophie, you are about to go into a dangerous enough place. Stay by me. As soon as we can, we shall leave. These women are the whores, when we are in the barracks you shall see the whore-mongers in red. Once they see you for what you are, they will want to marry you or earn from you. I am tempted to hide you in the bush but, with Staple running wild, that would not be safe either. Just stay quiet, act simple, and hopefully we shall leave this hell hole and be on our way very soon.' He sighed.

'But wouldn't they . . . '

'Sophie! No more questions!' his voice was so harsh she almost recoiled inside her loose coat. The realisation of the danger she was in hit her full force as she sat back, stroking the soldier's brow very gently whilst listening to the obscene cat calls that emanated from the factory as they passed by. Matthias was offered everything, yet he ignored all. There seemed to be a burden weighing his shoulders down. He had lost some of his spark, not his confidence, but it was like watching a free spirit succumb to being confined.

Sophie suspected he had been here before. This place haunted him as much as her past did her. She would never be trapped within a building again, answerable to an unyielding regime. She glanced back at the factory as they left it behind and every part of her flesh tingled, not in the warm way that Matthias had made it respond, but like ice running down her spine. Sophie would stay a free spirit. She saw the barracks ahead of them and a group of soldiers running with a cot towards the wagon. She also saw the triangle where people were flogged, and swallowed. She would remain free — she had to.

# 9

They drove the wagon up to the front of a long wooden building within the barracks. The injured man was then lifted between four soldiers down and into the main room where a table was cleared and he was unceremoniously laid out, ready for the doctor-cum-surgeon to inspect.

The doctor duly arrived. He pushed past Sophie and Matthias. Sophie noticed how grubby his hands were. She was glad that it was not her or Matthias who needed this man's attention. He looked rough — ignorant even, yet he held such an important position.

Matthias pulled her to his side as they looked in from the doorway. His eyes were on his wagon; hers were on the poor man who, not an hour earlier had been riding his lovely horse and who now laid motionless on the table in front of her. The doctor began to prod and poke his victim — patient.

'Come, we shall leave this place before the taste in my mouth makes me ill also.' He walked confidently back to the vehicle and climbed onto the seat, collecting the reins. Sophie did likewise.

'Hold!' the voice rang around the dusty square, which was in between the three long barrack buildings; the main office being centred between the living quarters and the jail and cookhouse. 'You there, you can't leave, there is a report to be prepared there are witness accounts to be completed and procedures to fulfil. You can't just ride off as if you were not party to this abominable event! You are not the law, sir. This is the law and that in there is a good man. His injuries are a travesty, an offence and the man responsible will be found and punished.' The man sniffed, he was short and was blustering, his cheeks flushed. He was obviously angered and upset that one of his men had been injured so.

'I was securing my wagon . . . sir. Besides, your sergeant saw the men attack me. He tried to knife me then spooked the poor man's horse, causing him to fall, before the brigand ran for his life into the bush. There is no more to tell than this. I have four days still to travel and would like to be on my way as soon as possible. With such a man at large I would like to put some distance between us and him as I can before I need to stop for the night again.' Matthias was controlling his temper and frustration, Sophie could tell by the manner of his speech, but the grip on the reins had tightened.

The sergeant stepped outside of the building. He had a solemn expression on his face. 'We're launching a manhunt. Staple is a now a murderer, sir. Lieutenant Jolly just left this world for a better place, I hope.'

The short man rushed back into the building, his eyes red.

'You saw what happened. You do not need me here. If we see him, if he crosses my path I will return him to you. Can we leave now?' He looked at the man.

'I know you, Wells. I remember you. You are arrogant and pompous. You never learned your lesson then and yet you still act as though you own this damned land.' His voice was cold. The soldier put a hand on the wagon near Sophie's leg, staring up under her hat at her face.

'You remember an injustice that was proved to be so, sir. My 'arrogance' was down to the injustices I suffered here and I have not forgotten any 'lessons'. They shall stay with me forever,' Matthias said quietly.

'Aye, perhaps so, but not before you'd tasted a Botany Bay dozen.' He placed his hand on Sophie's leg. She leaned into Matthias, instinctively. 'Twenty-five lashes tends to stay with a man, particularly a gentleman.' He grinned. 'I'll give you ten pounds for this one and you be on your way. That's a fair price for a filly fresh off the boats. I might even consider marrying her. What do you say, Wells?' He looked up at Matthias.

Sophie gripped his hand. She wanted to speak out, to protest, and to tell the man what he could do with his ten pounds but she remembered Matthias's words for her to stay silent — no matter what was said or happened. For once Sophie did as she had been told.

Matthias tensed. 'She is my wife!' He glared at the soldier who looked back at him surprised.

'Wise decision, Wells.' He slapped her thigh, and then stepped back. 'If you tire of her, bring her back here, I will still give you five pounds, no questions asked. So long as she is not with child. Now go, I know where your land is, if we need you, I shall see you and your 'lady' again. Be on your way, Wells, you got off last time, next time you might not be so lucky.' He turned away.

They walked the horse on, no sooner were they at the gates, when the sergeant with red eyes, came out of the building. 'Bring out the prisoner.' He had in his hand a cat of nine tails. Matthias flicked the reins and they increased the speed of the wagon. Sophie looked back, but then decided to do as Matthias did, and focussed on the road ahead. She pitied the thief for he was about to pay for what the runaway had done.

Behind them shouts could be heard. But it was not at them that the soldier was bawling his orders, it was to the hapless man who had tried to steal Matthias' parcel in the first place. The noises were soon drowned out by the cat-calling from the factory as they retraced their route, eventually leaving the town, passing the Governor's house.

Both were silent, both considered their own thoughts. Sophie had stayed close, nestled next to him on the seat. Once they were in the land of settlers where buildings were sparse and the country opened up again, she linked her arm through the crook of his elbow.

'We keep going until light is almost gone. We camp tonight with no fire and eat the bread and drink a little wine and leave early in the morning. If that man sees us we will be in great danger.' Matthias eventually shared his plan with her.

'Why did we not stay in a hotel until they caught him . . . ' she stopped talking as his head shot around, eyes staring directly at hers.

'Sophie, what will it take for you to heed the truth of the dangers you face in this land?'

'I only meant, that considering what you have just said, it would have possibly been the better of two evils,' she replied quietly. 'You would have been safer back there, wouldn't you?'

'You would have been in great danger staying there. I am only one man. I could not protect you if they had decided to throw me in jail overnight for questioning, or you too for that matter. However, they would not have been short of volunteers to interview you, Miss Dove.'

He wrapped an arm around her. She leaned her head against his shoulder and he rested his head on hers. 'What will you tell them if they ever come to your home and they find out that I am not your wife?'

'Sophie, they will not care if we are married or not. I was merely laying my claim to you so that he could not — not without creating further complications. Fortunately, for you, he had enough to deal with, as a murderer of a soldier on the loose takes priority over a bit of skirt.'

There was silence for a few moments. 'So I am coming with you to your farm.' She looked up at him wide-eyed, 'I mean, you want me to work for you? Like a housekeeper.'

'You are coming home with me, yes, Sophie.' He paused momentarily and Sophie thought that he had decided her future and she was to fall in with it. She felt as though she should revolt against it, but instead it made her feel wanted, secure and happy. When she made no comment he added. 'Where else can you go?' he asked, but Sophie knew it was a rhetorical question.

# 10

It was strange setting a camp with no fire. It was eerie. There were so many different sounds, movements surrounding her, and Matthias was ill at ease. She could sense his tension. They ate cold meat, dry bread and drank. It was they who were quiet whilst the creatures that were at peace in their land continued to make their songs, screeches or rustling noises as they had always done.

Sophie leaned back on the wagon and stared at the sky. It was beautiful and vast in her opinion. After the confines of the workhouse, the farm had felt like heaven, one where you had to work, but then she was used to that. However, after the stifling heat and cramped conditions upon the ship, this was yet another part of heaven she had never seen before. If it were not for the

brutality and harshness that her countrymen had brought to their shores,
how marvellous life here could be. She
dismissed thoughts of poisonous insects
and snakes as something she would
have to accept, like the mosquitoes or
illness, they were the natural hazards of
life. She set to and made her space in
the wagon as comfortable as she could.

Matthias walked over and took the
knife out from behind the driver's seat,
handing it to her.

'Keep this near you. Make sure it is
within the grasp of your hand and, if
you need to, do not hesitate to use it.'
He turned around to walk away again.

'Where are you going?' She tried not
to show the anxiety which she was
feeling, but her voice broke slightly as
she spoke.

'I shall not be far away. I will keep
watch.' He half smiled at her, his rifle
was held in his right hand. She knew he
was thinking of the man who had run
away, as if he was still a danger to them.
They could not move quickly, they had

a wagon to move. They could not hide their tracks for the same reason. Sophie realised they were an easy target.

'Matthias,' she used his Christian name, and he raised an eyebrow. 'You don't need to sleep on the ground without any fire. You can stay on the wagon. We will be safer together, won't we? I mean, it is better we keep together — for warmth, no fire.' She smiled at him, but her mouth trembled a little, realising that the offer could be seen as an open invitation, but she did not want to make things worse or more confused by trying to justify her words further.

He patted her shoulder. 'You sleep here; I will settle down where it will be best for both of us, once I am sure that we are alone. If I return and take you up on your appealing offer though, please be sure to open your eyes before you stab me with that knife of yours.'

'I would never . . . ' she began in her defence, but he winked at her and she realised he was only teasing her as if trying to calm her nerves with a little humour. She lay back, resting her head, but sleep would not come. Parramatta had made her realise how horrendous her life could have been if she had fallen as those unfortunate women had. Instead, she was here, safe, with Matthias. Whatever future they had together, the thought of sharing her life with him, as a housekeeper, pleased her immensely. Then another thought crossed her mind — strange that it had not before. He had said she was his wife. No one would care if she really was or just his common-law wife, his woman. Is that what he had decided? Had her offer for him to sleep with her for warmth confirmed this decision? She felt her cheeks flush. The thought of it caused her emotions to stir. The arrogance of a man is great, she understood this, so why should he be any different? The acceptance of such a situation, with no one there to say what was right or wrong would be a sin — temptation, but was it really wrong, out here, with only animals as neighbours? Surely, he would give her time to think about it. Had he survived out in the country, wherever he had lived, without company? Had he any? She had not asked and he had not said. There had been so little time together; most of their conversation had revolved around her questions, learning which tree was eucalyptus, mulberry, lemon or what strange animal, bird, insect made the latest fascinating sounds. He had told her of the rock oysters, cockles, turtles and shell fish that were found in the river. So she already knew the difference between the salt water parts and the inland river fish. Matthias had fascinated her with the talk of Dorak's people fishing with spears whilst the women used hooks sometimes made from shells. They had adapted nature to feed themselves.

Sophie had not asked about his family because she had felt intuitively that he was alone. The soldier had talked to him as if he had been accused and punished for a crime. What crime? She was in the middle of a vast new country, surrounded by danger, with only a flogged man to protect her. When she thought of it like that she realised that she did place her life in danger when she followed her instincts, but it was her way. To go against such feelings just seemed wrong.

Sophie dropped to sleep, but woke with an urgent need. She tried to ignore it, but the more she tried the more she realised she would have to find a bush. She peered over the side of the wagon. Automatically she stared into the darkness trying to see Matthias's shape asleep by the embers of the fire. There had been no fire. She could not make any shape of him out. Carefully, she collected the knife and climbed down over the back of the wagon. She did not want to go far, but Matthias had told her that she should not take a nature break too near where she slept, for it would attract creatures. She had not asked which creatures.

There was no movement other than hers. 'Matthias,' she whispered.

She waited a second but there was no reply. She took a deep breath. The sooner she did this the sooner she could return to her little place in the wagon, with held breath and swift an action as she could. She ventured ten paces away, placed the blade of the knife between her teeth and saw to her comfort. As soon as she was able she ran back to the wagon, almost leaping onto it, careful to hold the knife firmly in her grip lest she fall and cut herself or drop and lose it in the dark. It was as she dropped into her space that she landed on another body. She brought the knife around straight away. A man's hand clasped her wrist, forcing the knife down. His other arm was wrapped around her body, trapping her other arm to her side, whilst his mouth found hers. Sophie was flipped over, beneath him onto her back. The knife fell from her hand.

The urgency of the kiss, the musk she breathed in and the response from her own body told her all she needed to know. When he lifted his head slightly away from hers, she responded. 'Matthias Wells you nearly scared the life out of me. Do you realise what I could have done to you?'

She felt him laugh as his chest moved against her body.

'Release me, now!' she said firmly.

He placed the knife to one side under a bag, resting over her on one elbow; he looked down at her, flicking a strand of hair from her cheek.

'Do you not realise what I could have done to you if I had been a bushman or runaway. You left the wagon,' he continued to play with her hair as he talked. She was warm lying next to him.

'I had to . . . I needed to . . . ' she knew he was smiling at her.

'You needed to what?' he asked, and tenderly kissed her neck.

She moved gently, feeling like a cat purring but making no noise, as she tried to concentrate on admonishing him, not knowing where Matthias thought this moment of intimacy was going.

'Pee!' she snapped out, trying to wrong foot him again.

This time it did not work. He chuckled. 'Well done, you said a bad word.'

'You think . . . ' she began to reply, but he had other thoughts.

His lips found hers, whilst his hand slid, firmly and determinably, over the contours of her body until it rested upon her breast. Here it lingered. Sophie's arms embraced him. It was wrong; she knew by all that she had ever been told, that this behaviour was so wrong. However, her body, her mind and her instincts told her it was the most natural, beautiful thing in the world and she answered to no one — not even Matthias Wells.

Matthias had slid his rifle along the inside of the wagon when he had climbed in, waiting for Sophie to return. He had watched, discreetly to make sure she was in no danger. His hands, his mind, like the rest of his body were fully engaged elsewhere. Sophie felt the material of her belt being slowly loosened as their kiss intensified. She swallowed, not sure if this was wise, knowing that she was more than willing, beginning to doubt her own judgement, wondering if it was too late to say no; indecision clouding her brain, casting a mask over her feelings, her instinct lost in a whirl of heat and emotion.

She pulled her mouth from his, reluctantly. 'Matthias, we must stop, we must this is not wise.' Her hand found his, hardly covering the back of his, she held it firmly. He hesitated, lifted his head and looked at her, heavy lidded eyes, not wanting to break the moment, she knew. 'Not here, not now, not like this,' she smiled a little nervously at him. Her disappointment was as his own, but this was too rushed.

Matthias stopped instantly. There was no word of reply from him, no hesitation. One jolt of his body, shook her almost as much as it did him. An instant chill filled her as once more the moment was lost. So too had consciousness as his body slumped to the side of her, trapping her arm underneath his weight.

'Matthias . . . Matthias!' her voice was becoming louder until she saw a large figure loom over her. Benjamin Staple, with the knife in his hand, his own knife which he had recovered was standing at the side of the wagon peering down at her.

'No, lass, not 'ere, not now . . . but soon enough.' He slapped her thigh. 'Now get out here and help me with the nags,' he ordered, stepping back, whilst gesturing with the knife towards Matthias.

'Is he . . . dead?' she asked, and leaned toward him, but Staple put the blade to the back of Matthias' neck and glared at her. 'Get out or I'll make sure he is.' The palm of his hand rested on the end of the handle of the knife, the tip against Matthias' skin.

'He will be if you don't do as I say. Move!' he shouted. Sophie tugged her arm free, trying not to disturb Matthias' position as Staple kept the blade on his neck. Sophie forced the panic back down so she would not cry, but her heart was aching to know if Matthias was going to be all right. She had not time to consider her own plight. She knew only too well that so long as he had to run, she was safe, until he stopped, then she would be in danger. For he would not stop until he felt safely away from his pursuers, the soldiers from the barracks who wanted him for the murder of one of their own. He was a marked man like no other. Once they stopped running fate would take over as it always had. She had to stay strong for Matthias.

She stepped down from the wagon, glancing sadly at Matthias, her heart aching with fear for his safety, but she did as she was told. She had no choice for both of their sakes. He grabbed the material at the back of her coat and roughly pulled it from her, leaving her in her shirt and breeches. He tossed the garment in the wagon and continued to half drag her over to where Matthias's horse was tethered.

'Get up on it, and no tricks!' he snapped.

'My coat,' Sophie began to speak. She rubbed one arm along the fabric of her other sleeve. She felt strangely exposed, knowing there was only the fabric of her shirt between her body and this man.

'It will be in the way, my way — up!' he gestured with the knife for her to mount the horse, his eyes stared, hard and unyielding. She hated him.

Sophie had no choice; she put one foot in the stirrup and was appalled when he roughly pushed her rump upward. Before she was sitting straight in the saddle he had mounted the animal behind her. He put the knife in the back of his belt, gripped the reins around her with his right hand, pinning her to him with his left. She could feel his grip holding her to him, smelling his foul breath on her neck as he kicked the horse on. Tears welled up in her eyes. His touch was so rough, so coarse unlike the caress of Matthias. He revolted her. The man had injured or killed Matthias, she had deserted him to God alone knew what creatures, and the murderer had her firmly in his grasp.

Without time to look back again they rode away at speed and all Sophie could do was pray.

# 11

Matthias awoke from unconsciousness and he hurt. He hurt so badly that for a moment he thought the darkness had held him a prisoner, but then realised his eyes were still tightly shut as he grimaced against the pain. He moved his head and rubbed his face. A sharp ache speared down from his temple into his head, like needles penetrating his skull. His senses were confused; he felt the objects that were scattered around him. Hessian bags, coiled rope, tools, wood, no body, no one else there. Matthias remembered feeling warm, feeling someone . . . feeling . . . Beatrice? She had left him again, he was alone. He slumped for a moment knowing this was not right, realising he was forgetting something . . . someone, trying to place together the pieces of his life. He heard an animal move; a horse whinnied. Feeling the hard board beneath his body as he tried to force himself upright, he muttered a word. 'Wagon!'

Matthias pushed down with his hands until he was teetering on his knees and slowly opened his eyes. The world around him spun as he regained his focus. 'Sophie!' he said. Holding the side of the wagon he steadied himself as he peered out into the surrounding area, straining to see where she was.

He leaned over the side; his world swirled again, so he straightened his back. The crown of his head was damp and a swelling was coming up. It hurt, but he knew he would have been in more trouble if the swelling had gone inward. He would repay the man who did it, and that man, he believed, was Staple. Matthias swore that he would see justice done. He lifted his leg over the side of the wagon and slid it down to the earth. Feeling the land beneath his foot he carefully placed the other one next to it, whilst still holding on tightly to the vehicle. He felt around inside the wagon with his right hand, searching for his rifle. It was still there. Fortunately, his body had obscured it from his attacker's view, but the knife and pistol had gone. This told him Staples was in a hurry to be away. He was a hunted man and they did not stop. What worried him was that he had been prepared to burden himself with Sophie. Matthias reasoned that Staple was heading deep into the bush and was planning to hide out for some time. Perhaps even make his way further north. Did he want a woman's company? Did he want to sell her on to gain easy cash from other bushrangers or runaways or was he planning to take her far enough away with him to reap his revenge and then murder her? Matthias had no way of knowing which option the man would take, but all were abhorrent; he had to help her before it was too late.

Looking around he felt doubly sad, for not only had he lost his woman, but he realised his horse had gone too. Matthias' head cleared for a moment as he stood still, thinking that that was how he thought of her. Sophie clearly liked him; he could see in her eyes a softness there, the look that said he warmed her soul when she looked at him. Her body definitely responded to his touch. Matthias wanted her, he wanted to be more than just a man to her, and deep inside his own soul he still wanted the love of a good woman. He had not found one easily and had given up the search, hoping against hope that in desperation he would avoid the need of searching one out from the factory, souls destroyed or hardened whether guilty or not of a wrong. Then he had seen her, lost and confused on the quayside in Sydney, helping the lad. Not many would; few women would have stood so close to the native boy. They would normally scream in ignorance at their own paranoia of his kind.

The recollection of that first sighting of Sophie looking so lost brought anger into his head, blotting out the nagging pain which had started to creep back into his brain. Although not as sharp as when he first woke, it was still there. He felt the back of his head and touched dried blood. 'Damn the man!' He had an open wound, not that big, but any such wound left unattended could become diseased and dangerous. He tried to think what he had with him that could help to stop it going bad. Matthias felt around for his canteen. He needed to clean it at least.

'You hurt badly, mister?'

The voice was so sudden and unexpected that Matthias spun around, lost his balance and found himself flat on the floor. The jolt sent a searing pain through his head. His hand fumbled around desperately at the earth trying to grasp a stone, stick or anything he could reach in order to save himself further harm.

Matthias started to inch his way up to his knees. He could not find any makeshift weapon. His wits, addled as they were, would have to suffice. Kneeling, staring about him, he could not see anyone. Yet he knew the voice had been real enough. Who was playing games with him? The voice sounded strange; it was not a man's and yet not that of a woman or a young child. He needed to track Sophie's kidnapper, but the daylight was not there yet. Time was passing. She was in danger and now so was he — again. Matthias had protected her so far, but had let her be kidnapped like that, whilst he slept. He was near to despair. Matthias blamed his own stupidity for the situation they were in, for if he had only waited until they were home, she would be safe and their union would not have been so rushed. His gut turned at the thought of her being hurt in anyway.

Despite Beatrice, despite swearing never to trust another female again, he had warmed to Sophie's spirit, her innocence, and he wanted to protect that above all else. For if he could relearn how to view this land as he once had, a land filled with beauty and challenge, then he could also learn to live again filled with ambition, life and love. She had rekindled Matthias' spirit. She had reminded him that he once had a dream and that it was still there, somewhere hidden away in his soul. It had not died with Beatrice. The hurt and the grief both gnawed at him as he stood tall again, one hand on the wagon's side and one on the rifle. The past had gone. If he wanted a future he had to find Sophie. First, he had to trace the owner of the voice and find out if they were a friend or a foe?

'You give Dorak the gun, mister, and I see your head not go bad.' The voice was above him — no, behind him. The boy from the harbour was on the wagon.

He had yanked the rifle from Matthias' loose grip and dropped it behind him in the wagon. He held something in his other hand. Matthias did not know what the mixture was, but it smelt and looked foul.

134

'Head down, mister, and I stop your head from going on its own journey to your spirit world, leaving your body to rot here on its own.'

'You have a way of putting things which is very descriptive. What is it?' he asked.

'Your life. You want it or you want to lose it?' The lad waited.

Matthias rested his head against the side of the wagon and felt the mixture being pressed carefully against the point where his skull felt as though it had been split. He knew that the natives could use plants and the animals in their surroundings as medicine, and his options were few. He had to trust the lad knew what he was doing, to use Sophie's reasoning. His instinct told him he needed to.

'Why help me? You could have stolen the wagon and been away, leaving me here. The soldiers would think Staple had taken it.' Matthias spoke quietly, not knowing why he was rambling and asking such a stupid question. The lad would have no need of most of the things on it and he would be strung up for theft if he tried to sell any of it. The soldiers would track the wagon before they found Sophie or Staple.

'You helped me and Yani back there,' he replied. 'You saved my skin, now I save yours. Lie in the wagon and sleep. You better not move before morning.'

'Yani?' Matthias asked, wondering if he had had another friend with him who Matthias had missed. If so, he was not the man he once was.

'The woman. You careless, you lost her to a bad man.' There was a note of reproof in his words.

Matthias tried to lift his head, but Dorak had his hand over his wound still. 'I have to find her. She needs me.'

'She needed you before, now you injured. You stay; you sleep till morning and then follow the tracks which I will leave. You can do that mister. I make them easy. I find her tonight. You give me the rifle and I help her, and then bring her back here for you.'

'You expect me to trust you with my rifle?' Matthias heard him chuckle. 'You know how valuable that is out here?'

'What of Yani? Has she no 'value' to you?' his voice was hard, critical, bitter even.

'I don't put value on humans. I leave that to others. It is just that we need to protect ourselves.' Matthias did not want to admit he had an attachment to his gun, because it had saved his life many times in the Peninsular. That was part of his past. The sailor had judged him wrong in the alley. He was never a navy man, but a soldier, a rifleman and that was in a previous life, or so it felt to him. The rifle was the only link left to that existence and the man he had been.

'Do you trust the bushman with your woman?' the boy asked.

'No!' Matthias was angry, tired and frustrated.

'Then trust me. I bring her here safe and then you let me stay on the land you call your land, in peace.'

'My land is my own!' Matthias snapped.

'My country has been stolen. My people were killed. You need help. I need peace — I need Yani, she is my friend. She teaches me your ways. You stay here and I get her.' He released the pressure from Matthias' head and placed his hat carefully over it.

'Unhitch the horse. I am coming with you,' his words were confident. He raised his eyes to meet those of the boy. 'You help me, we save her and I will give you a home and your peace.' He held the boy's stare, deep brown determined eyes met in a test of strength of wills.

Dorak smiled. 'Good, then we go. He is in the creek. I know where he is heading, but I know how to get there quickly.'

# 12

Together they worked to cover the wagon up, hiding it and disguising the tracks as far away from the road as they could. Then they unhitched the horse. Matthias' wound felt numb. He had asked Dorak to bind the crown of his head with a piece of cloth from the stores in the wagon, leaving the poultice to work its wonders undisturbed underneath. His hat was placed carefully over this. Once the sun shone down he would need the brim. He knew he was not as sharp as he would normally be, but he was able to ride without a saddle and, as the numbness removed his pain, he focussed on what he had to do.

Dorak insisted on going on foot, leading the way in front of Matthias. They picked their way for what seemed to Matthias like hours. Daylight broke and the heat increased as the morning lengthened before them, and still they continued. Matthias fought the tiredness which threatened to overtake him. Then, Dorak stopped and raised his hand.

'You leave the horse here. We go on foot. You load rifle. If your head is bad still, then I shoot, if necessary, Mister Wells.' He stood confidently staring at Matthias.

'You give orders well,' Matthias said, as he swung his right leg over the saddle, removing his left foot from the stirrup, and slid down off the horse, not taking his eyes from Dorak. He saw a half smile on the boy's face.

'You don't trust even someone who has helped you. You people don't trust your own shadows.' The bitterness in his voice, and the hatred within his eyes, surprised Matthias. 'You only know how to hurt and kill.'

Matthias walked over to him. 'Tell me, your people, your family, were they all killed in the uprising three months back? Were they?' he asked.

Dorak nodded. He could not hold Matthias' stare, his head tilted downwards and Matthias saw by the tear that fell on the earth next to Dorak's foot that he had guessed correctly. He placed a hand on the youth's shoulder.

'Then I am ashamed of what my countrymen have done to your people and what happened there, but you will learn we are not all the same. I will give you a home, but you must help me now. Sophie — your 'Yani' — needs our help and we have to work together. I do not want her to be hurt and I have let her down badly, Dorak. I will trust you, unless you prove my faith misplaced, but you must promise that if I take you to my home that you will never touch the grog or rum. You stay clear of that stuff and trouble will stay away from you.'

Dorak's head shot up. 'I won't. My word!'

Matthias nodded. 'I keep the rifle because I will not hesitate to use it if I have to. Believe me, Dorak, I know how to kill, but only in defence and for a good reason. Even with a lump on my head I can take the eye out of a kookaburra at a hundred paces.' Matthias bragged to try to give the boy some confidence in him.

Dorak smiled. 'Then we shall hope for Yani's sake that she was stolen away by a noisy bird, mister.' He turned and started to make his way through the bush.

Matthias followed thinking to himself that if they succeeded in their mission he would not be lonely again. He seemed to have collected more than basic supplies from Sydney. Matthias had the makings of a family. That thought stirred others. His own family would not approve of either the workhouse girl or the aborigine, but then they had never approved of anything he did, not since the flogging, and then Beatrice. As he silently followed the boy along, he also realised he didn't care what they thought anymore. Sophie was his concern now and that was all he needed to focus on . . . well, except for the lad. He held the loaded rifle in his hand, and moved swiftly through the bush behind Dorak. Memories of many a skirmish filled his mind, when Dorak stopped he hid. He pointed out to Matthias, an old shack ahead of them in what had once been a clearing. Someone had obviously tried to make a home here and failed. The land around it, once tilled, had grown back to a more natural state. The shack's roof was in need of repair, but it would be enough to hide out in, if you were desperate. Matthias squatted next to him.

'If I go inside and wait, can you cover my tracks? You take my horse away as soon as he is inside and I will see that she is not hurt.' Matthias saw he was thinking the suggestion over. He tilted his head back, listening.

Matthias knew the same tricks. No matter where the land was, when it was your home, if you listened to the animals and the noises of the forest, you could tell when danger was nearing.

'Quick, mister.'

Matthias ran over to the shack. He paused long enough to listen a moment by the door. With the tip of his rifle's barrel he pushed the wood. It creaked as it swung open. Dust from the earth outside on the threshold showed there were no fresh foot prints. If this was where she was being brought, and he prayed the boy had judged the situation correctly, then they had not arrived as yet. He took a leap inside so as not to leave a boot print and walked into the dark shadows of the interior.

He did not see Dorak, but sensed the boy was busy covering his tracks. Matthias could make out a narrow bed of sorts against the far wall. A makeshift stove was rusting away in the centre and a few pots were scattered around the edge of the walls. It was dusty, dry and stale inside, but he did not want to leave the door open wide as that would look odd. So he stayed stock still, listening for any sound within which might hint that he was not alone. Snakes were the main danger, other than Staple when he arrived.

\*   \*   \*

Sophie fought to keep her calm. Staple held her close to him, one hand controlling the horse as he led it along the path of a creek. They had ridden for hours. Gradually the man's anxiety had relaxed. For most of the journey he had held her as if in a vice, his strong hand firmly against her ribcage. The other arm held the reins. They followed the line of the creek. His body seemed to relax as if he knew the place and was aware they had reached somewhere of relative safety. This was when Sophie tensed. Now, was her time of danger. He began to nuzzle her neck. His mouth slobbering over her skin. She leaned as far away as she could but then she felt his teeth begin to bite, and she yelped. This made him laugh.

'No! No! Not now, not yet . . . not

here,' he mimicked her words, only where hers had been of a gentle request, he turned them into a pathetic plea, as they rode along. His hand slid from her side to her breast. She could feel the heat of his palm through the fabric of the shirt. She felt as though naked, revealed, defiled. He groped for her breast roughly and his mouth was there again like a leech upon her skin. Sophie wriggled but his grip was firm. The more she resisted the harder he grabbed or bit. She kicked the horse's sides hard, not wanting to hurt the animal but desperate to be free. Once he stopped and dragged her from the horse all would be lost, as he was too strong for her to fight fairly. So she surprised and hurt the horse, praying it would react violently. It did, the animal bolted at speed. He had to hold the reins with both hands in order to control it. They lost the path, strange trees poked and snatched at their clothes. He swore, words that Sophie had never heard before, but she did not care. His hands were off her body. She jostled around within his arms as he fought to bring the animal back into control. If he did now, she knew her punishment would be the worse for her actions.

'Get out of my way. Duck your head you stupid bitch! You trying to kill us?' She saw a branch ahead which was across their path. Now was her chance. She ducked just as they approached it. It missed her, but hit him full on the face, drawing blood and sending him backwards off the horse. The animal reared and she also fell. She landed on her back, taking her breath away. She was able to curl into a ball as she was thrown, protecting her head from the force of the landing. Quickly, she uncoiled and stood. He was on his feet already, but instead of running for her he was trying to retrieve the frightened horse. She ran amongst the wilderness, not knowing where she was heading, but so long as a horse could not get there then that would be fine. She just wanted to put as much distance as she could between her body and his hands and his stinking breath. Somehow, she had to know how to return to Matthias. She tried to look at the direction of the sun. It was what she had been doing since they left. Sophie would feel lost alone if she had the time to think of her own plight, but she did not. Matthias' life depended upon her being able to return to him. As she ran, she blotted out the panic which rose within her when the thought that it may be too late occurred to her. She knew he lived. Her instinct told her he did and it was never wrong.

She crouched down and waited as she heard hooves the other side of the bushes some ten feet away. Her shirt had been ripped on her sleeve, but fortunately, although a barb had scratched her; it had not cut her skin. Sophie froze as her eyes saw movement to her right: a black snake slid by not two feet from where she crouched. She held her breath and did not dare to move. If it had been

Matthias out there she would have cried for help, but it was not. The man she hid from scared her more than this creature. Transfixed, she watched the strange movement of its muscles as it appeared to glide along, noticing the pretty red under its belly. It also heard the movement of the horse and hissed. She stayed still, thinking that if she made no attempt to hurt it, it may just keep going by without trying to hurt her. It was heading towards the creek and as it responded to the noise of the animal riding past, it seemed to move all the more quickly. She watched in awe as the head was followed by a body some four or so feet in length. Sophie's instincts served her well again. It went on its way. She stayed perfectly still, except from a steady shaking inside her tummy, realising that Staple was doing the same. He was playing a waiting game. If she moved then she would give herself away. So she closed her eyes and prayed again. It was what she did when all else failed. After what seemed like endless minutes she heard the horse walk away. Still she did not move until in the distance she heard the hooves of a galloping horse become fainter. Then, she stood up, and smiled. Looking around her the smile faded. She was completely lost. She knew nothing of the land, the creatures, and had nothing to eat or drink. It was hot and getting hotter, all she could do was try and retrace her tracks until she found the wagon and hope that no one or nothing would prevent her from returning to Matthias. So she started to walk wondering if she cried would she dehydrate more quickly than her instinct told her she was going to. Sophie hoped above all hopes that this time instinct would be wrong and God would save her from her own foolishness. She should never have let Matthias settle with her in the wagon. It was what she had wanted and she felt like Eve, temptation had led to their fall. For an awful moment her spirit felt burdened and crushed.

A bird flew up from a bush near her. It was beautiful, full of colour and song.

She could not help but smile. How could she die here when the place was so full of life. She loved this strange bewildering land, she loved Matthias and it was not wrong to want him and to be with him. This was all God's creation; it was men like Staple who made it bad, and the people in authority who beat the goodness out of their victims in the name of justice, reducing them to little more than animals. So were they the reason that Staple existed? Too many questions and two many thoughts. She hummed her own birdsong, a ditty from her childhood, and quickened her step. The tracks were fresh still. Benjamin Staple had headed the opposite way, so now she could return to the wagon and all would be well again — she hoped.

★ ★ ★

Matthias felt the sweat on his forehead. He waited, until his reward came. He heard the horse approaching. Standing

151

against the wall in the shadows of the shack he stayed calm. His rifle was loaded, it was poised ready, but he was expecting the man to open the door and throw Sophie inside. Instead Staple's figure entered. He dropped a saddle bag on the bed, and turned as the gun was cocked behind him.

'What have you done with her?' Matthias asked.

The man spun around bewildered.

'How . . . '

The rifle was raised, aimed and ready.

# 13

'So you managed a miracle!' Staple spoke boldly, his calm manner impressing Matthias, yet only serving to show just how hard a rock the man was. 'I should have used the knife instead of the pistol butt. It was such a touching scene with the two of you that I hardly wanted to interrupt. If you had not set the army on me, I wouldn't be running now. I worked hard to gain a ticket-of-leave and you damn well cost me it, my only friend and, if they catch me, then it will be my life. So you can see, I is a desperate man — that means desperate measures. You can see what a problem you give me.'

Matthias could see the shiftiness in Staple's eyes. He kept his rifle sight straight on him.

'Where is Sophie?' he asked with cold contempt and barely controlled anger.

'You really should take better care and control of your woman.' Staple laughed. 'Don't you know the first rule of survival in this place? You should never turn your back on an enemy, man, but you forgot such a simple thing as you were so busy.' He chuckled, until the rifle pointed at his head. 'Shoot me down, murder me in cold blood and you will never know what happened to her, will you?' He sneered.

'If you have hurt her then a swift death is what you will beg me for.' Matthias glared at him. 'Drop the knife and pistol or I will blow what brains you have out of your head.'

The door flew open, nearly hitting Matthias in his side. 'Where is Yani?' the boy screamed at Staple from the doorway.

Matthias was taken by surprise by this sudden action, as the lad shouted his words. In that split second Matthias's advantage was lost. His surprise had been usurped by Dorak's emotional plea. Matthias swore to himself as

Staple was quick to react, grabbing the light frame of the boy by his arm, holding Dorak in front of him with the knife blade's point to the boy's neck.

Matthias held the rifle firmly, he did not let the sight of his rifle waver. He could see the fear in the lad's eyes; one bullet would take Staple down but he wanted to — needed to know what he had done to Sophie. Damn the boy's impatience! he thought.

'Well, now. We have ourselves a pretty situation. Drop the gun or I'll skin the boy.' Staple snapped, yanking Dorak's head back, exposing his neck to the threat of the knife.

'So, what if you do? One less to steal sheep, so where is the wench?' Matthias kept a cold, detached tone to his voice. He could see the hatred in the wide-eyes of the frightened youth. Matthias hoped he would hold on to what trust he had in him.

'You don't keep account of your friend's fella, nor your women.' Staple lifted the boy to his feet turning the scruff of his neck tight so that to struggle or fight would mean certain death from the blade. 'You put the gun down. If he helped you, and he obviously has or you would not be here, then you won't want any harm to come to him. Think I'm simple, do you? You couldn't find your way here without his kind, not that quick. Lower the gun; you aren't the sort to want his blood on your hands. Not after you losing the wench so easy when you were just getting so cosy like. Well, don't you worry, because she wasn't to be disappointed. I made sure she knew what she was missing and mighty grateful she was too — she died laughing!' He grinned widely as the lad sobbed, and Matthias' eyes showed the disgust and hatred he felt.

His words had the impact he intended, striking like the cut of the knife at Matthias's heart. Matthias swallowed, he did not want to believe the man's boast. He didn't want to think of her hurt, broken and abandoned. The effect that his lies had on the boy were devastating to see. Staple took advantage of the moment. He propelled the boy straight at Matthias, but, as he released Dorak, Matthias fired a bullet so that it went straight into its target. The man fell back with one solitary wound in his head. Dorak gasped and stared up at Matthias before running towards the door. Matthias, knowing what his intention was, held his arms tightly before he could make it to the outside world and disappear into the bush.

'You're like all of them. I mean nothing to you. You'd let him fillet me like a fish. You're evil!' the words poured out of Dorak's mouth, heated by emotion and fuelled by hate and disappointment.

'You believe that?' He held him at arm's length so that he could look into his eyes. 'Dorak, I had to call his bluff. If I'd put the gun down we would both be dead now. I need you to track Sophie down. I need you to find her. She lives. If he had stopped long enough to do what he said he had, he would not have been here so soon. She must have broken free of him. He was taunting me to distract me; I don't believe she is dead. Listen to me, Dorak!' He was almost shaking the boy to bring him back to his senses.

'You think she lives?' The boy had tears flowing down his cheeks.

'Yes, I really do, but if she is on foot, if she is running frightened in the bush she will need you to find her tracks. Dorak, think clearly, her life depends upon your skills. Where do we go?'

The boy nodded. He obviously saw the sense in Matthias' words. 'I find her. I find her with your help. This time we both ride. If she is on foot, very dangerous for a white woman . . . Very dangerous she has no water, mister. Come, but you don't do that to me again.'

Matthias hesitated looking at Staples.

'Leave him for the animals. Put him in the bush, they will remove the evidence of his death. Let the soldiers find his bones.' Dorak's words were bitter. 'Do it. He was one that attacked my people. I know,' Dorak spoke as he walked to the body, bent down and untied a piece of woven cloth from Staples belt. 'This tells me all I need to know. Leave him as he left my people.'

Matthias considered this for a moment. It made sense. It was not what he would have normally done which should have been to return the body to the barracks with his account of events. However, time was of the essence and he had no desire to be accused of murder. His own name had been besmirched. Quickly he lifted Staples and deposited him by the creek. The soldiers would not believe he killed him to save a boy such as Dorak. They would be doubly angry that they had been denied their own vengeance. Matthias, thus justified, did Dorak's bidding and did not look back.

They both mounted Matthias' horse, returned to where Matthias had tied the wagon's animal which Dorak climbed on. They then retraced Staples tracks to a place where footprints emerged, and it was obvious that something had happened here.

Dorak dismounted and scouted around. He stopped and shook his head. 'Yani was here.' He then pointed to a pattern on the ground which Matthias knew too well. 'So was snake. Red belly. Not good, but not stopped. I think she went that way. She very lost.'

He remounted and they followed, having to move slowly because to go any faster would be to miss her tracks.

Matthias was aware of a dull ache in his head, but it had improved. He was too busy thinking about finding Sophie to ponder on it. Once she was safe then he would rest. Until then, he would carry on.

★　★　★

Matthias rode the horse carefully through the bush, following the tracks that Staple had made when he kidnapped Sophie. They were difficult to follow but Matthias had been on too many skirmishes when he was serving Wellington to be fooled by any tricks the like of Staple used. He listened to what seemed a strange bird sound from a distance, but then as he approached he realised it was not a bird that was singing. This song he had heard before, it was a voice he knew and a smile played on his lips until he saw Sophie's dusty figure in the distance. Wearing her hat, shirt and breeches she was walking along humming to herself. A more beautiful image he had never seen. He dismounted, quickly securing the horse, and ran to her.

Because she had been watching the ground and retracing her tracks she did not see him at first. It was only when she heard the rush of his feet as he neared that she looked up startled, until she recognised his figure. Then she too ran.

'Matthias!' she yelled, as she swung

her arms around him. He lifted her into the air and kissed her as if he was possessing her very soul. He held her tightly to his body feeling hers through the fabric of her shirt, standing there just hugging her until he realised she needed a drink, then his lips parted from hers and her feet slipped back down to the earth. He reached for his canteen and let her taste the much needed fluid.

★ ★ ★

Her thirst temporarily sated, Sophie wrapped her arms around his waist and hung on to him like a limpet to a rock. He still lived; they both had survived and were safe. Her instinct had served her well once more. 'I'm sorry!' she said, as she held back unshed tears. 'I did not want to leave you. I was so scared that I feared you would be eaten by creatures or robbed or already dead.'

'It was I who should apologise to you. I should never have let my guard down. I have more experience than that.' He patted her shoulder as, in the distance; another rider appeared along the track. 'We both owe our thanks to someone else,' Matthias said, and then pointed to Dorak who was slowly walking the horse towards them. 'He may well have saved my life, and his ability to read this land helped to lead me to you.'

Sophie wiped her eyes with the back of her hand. 'Dorak!' She walked over to welcome her 'secret' friend. 'However did you find me? I thought that you would have been miles away with your own people by now?' He did not answer her, instead he glanced at Matthias. Sophie sensed something was wrong so she changed the subject quickly. She could find out later from Matthias what tragedy had brought Dorak back to her. 'Where is Staple? Did the soldiers catch him?'

Dorak had been smiling until she had asked about his family, and then mentioned the bushranger's name. Then his smile left him to be replaced by a strange stare which was still directed toward Matthias. She looked to him also. Something devastating must have happened to her happy friend to make him so aggrieved. Sophie felt for him. He seemed strangely alone.

'He is no more of a threat to you or anyone. We were all lucky. Now, we shall hitch up the wagon again, drink more and refresh ourselves, and then we shall make our way to my home. From now on it will be a home to all of us.' He took Sophie by the hand and led her to his horse. Placing both hands firmly on her waist he lifted her up, and then climbed up behind her. 'Come, Dorak, don't be afraid anymore. You are with me now.'

The boy followed on behind them but there was a sadness to him which Sophie knew had not been there before. When he was on board the ship he had been fired by the hope of returning. Now that hope had gone. He had been so excited at the thought of going back home and escaping the ship. Perhaps this had been one adventure too many for him.

On the way back to the wagon Matthias explained how Dorak had found him, rescued him and helped him to track Staple down. Sophie listened and shared her side of events missing out the detail of Staple's assault upon her which had triggered her rash and desperate action of spooking the horse.

Before they set off to travel down the road and continue their journey, Dorak and Sophie cleaned Matthias' head, removing the remnants of the clay based poultice and as both were satisfied it would heal well, he replaced his hat.

'Sophie, I want you to wear your dress as we go to my home. We will be stopping at my father's home first and I would have him look upon you with respect. It is time you were a young lady again, at least for a while.'

Sophie felt a little disappointed. She had enjoyed travelling, riding and running in breeches. Her movements were so much more athletic and her actions free. The thought of wearing a dress just did not thrill her at all. 'You gave my travel dress away and my best dress is not suitable.' Her excuse was feeble she knew it, but she wanted to stay as she was.

He leaned into the wagon and pulled a small parcel to her. 'Try this instead.'

She stared wide-eyed at it. Opening the paper so carefully as if that was a precious part of the gift, she unfolded it to reveal a pale lemon dress of a much lighter cotton, not at all suitable for working in. He then pulled out of a roll a hat made of a straw-like material, which sprang into the shape of a simple wide-brimmed hat.

'You change into those in the wagon.' He looked at Dorak. 'We shall look the other way. If you go toward the box at the end you will see a pair of shoes. These I bought in Sydney; they will be your calling clothes. You will not use them often, but as for my father, I want him to see a respectable young woman or he will presume you to be my concubine.' He looked at her confused face. 'Mistress . . . whore, Sophie.' He smiled at her.

'Oh,' she said, her cheeks flushing beneath the sunburn which unavoidably she had caught upon her face as she had walked, checking the position of the sun to make sure she was still going the right way. It was something Dorak had told her when they were on the ship. He was excellent at navigation because he read the sky. He knew how to watch the moon, stars and the sun like a map.

She climbed into the back of the wagon. Dorak sat next to Matthias, who winked at him reassuringly.

'Tell me, mister. What do you suggest I wear so that your pa won't think ill of me?' his eyes had the same lifeless stare as he had when he talked of his family and Staple.

Matthias let out a long low whistle. 'You stay quiet unless I ask you something directly, then answer respectfully.

You stay with me or Sophie and you don't do or say anything rash. In western terms he is very well educated, here he is ignorant and it is you who has the knowledge. Do not flaunt it, just stay humble. We won't be staying in the house for long.'

Dorak nodded. 'I do a good humble.'

# 14

'Matthias,' Sophie said, once dressed in her new finery. This dress had not been worn before. It was a little loose, but that suited her fine, because it was so hot. To own a dress with no patches or darns in a material that did not itch or pinch almost brought tears to her eyes. Matthias glanced back as she was combing out her hair before pinning it under her bonnet.

His glance became a long lingering look. Dorak took the reins from his hands as he moved to face her.

Unaware of the attention she was getting, Sophie turned towards him happy that her hat was secure. She saw the smile on his face and knew that he approved of this attire more than her breeches. She was flattered but she did not. 'Why don't you rest in the back and we can lead the wagon?' she asked.

He smiled. 'Believe me, I would happily climb in the back right now, but you do not know where we are going, and I am the one they will recognise. You rest and I shall tell you when we are near.'

Sophie did not argue. She rolled up her clothes making a pillow and lay back, content with the motion of the wagon, listening to the chatter between Dorak and Matthias. How strange she thought life was. They were totally different yet shared the same love for the land. It was good to hear Matthias talk so animatedly about the country and the land he had built his home on. She realised that Dorak had rekindled a love for it in him, which had been missing only days before. How quickly time can change things.

When the wagon stopped Sophie rejoined Matthias and Dorak sat in the wagon.

'It won't be for long, Dorak, but keep in the background whilst I make the introductions.'

The road branched. They followed a wide track which led to land that had been cleared and marked by a letter **'W'** on the boundary trees. It was a symbol of ownership which had always made Matthias feel proud, but with Dorak's silence, it made him feel a little uneasy for the first time. However, his and his father's blood and sweat had carved out this estate from virgin wilderness and he was not going to relinquish that. Matthias' back straightened.

Sophie sat amazed at the transformation from wilderness, to clearance, to grass. In an oasis of colonial life was laid a huge lawn in the middle of which had been built a large house with a veranda around the main building. Men worked around the edges of the estate, ticket of leave, she presumed. The building had been painted white. It was remarkable, yet strangely out of place, she thought.

A few of the workers who they passed by tipped their hats respectfully at

Matthias, their eyes scanning Sophie, showing unvoiced appreciation, which dropped from their expressions when they saw Dorak.

After more minutes a stable block came into sight, and out buildings. Further over behind the house were a collection of smaller huts, where it seemed a small colony existed of farm hands and their families. Sophie realised that, if this was Matthias' home, she would have no standing here, for he must be of the gentry and as a workhouse orphan, she was marginally higher in society's eyes than the boy in the back of the wagon. What was the word Matthias had used? Concubine. She wondered if that was the best she could hope to be to the man she had fallen in love with.

He pulled the wagon up in front of the veranda. There were even a few rose bushes planted. Stepping down, he retrieved a parcel from the back and then came to Sophie. He offered her his hand so that she may at least step onto the veranda as a lady would. He nodded to Dorak to follow, and then shouted to one of the hands to see to the horses, but to leave the wagon there for the time being.

They rubbed their feet on a clip mat just inside the door. Matthias led them into a room which was sparse of furniture except for a few tall backed leather covered chairs, a table with a map weighted down upon it, and a wall covered with shelves which were half full of books. It looked like a reading room in the making, to Sophie.

In the corner, standing by the window, was a gentleman dressed in the fashion of position, Sophie thought. His sombre expression and grey hair told her he could well be Matthias' father.

'You bought the tobacco and collected my books?' the man said dryly, apparently ignoring the presence of Sophie.

Matthias placed the parcel on the table in front of him. 'Father, this is Miss Sophie Dove. She is a governess recently arrived from England.'

She smiled politely at him, nodding her head slightly, not sure if she should have curtseyed or not.

He opened the parcel and checked the contents, seemingly reassured that they were in good order. He then glanced at her, before staring at his son. 'You are too old for a governess, Matthias.' His eyes saw Dorak. 'Don't tell me that you have adopted him and employed her in one simple trip for supplies.'

'Why would I tell you such a thing, Father? Miss Dove will be staying with me and so will the boy. Her position was not 'suitable'. I aim to offer her a better one.'

His father walked over to Sophie. 'You are younger than the last one. Did he tell you what happened to her? Hmm?' He raised his eyes.

'I knew this would be folly. I have delivered your things. We will eat, wash and find a new horse for the wagon and then I will be on my way. I will be using the lodge as our home. Don't worry I shall extend the boundary to farm my own land. Your land will not be tainted by my presence anymore than it has been already.' Matthias placed a hand under Sophie's elbow to walk her out.

'That is it then, is it? You walk in here with your menagerie and calmly walk back out. Have you dealt with your past son? Does it haunt you?' Matthias looked at the floor, he side-glanced at Sophie, his face flushed. She felt his hand which seemed slightly clammy and realised he was running a temperature.

'Sir, he is unwell!' she said, and looked at the father knowing the son's eyes were fixed upon her.

'I am fine!' he snapped, but Dorak swept his hat from his head, revealing the cut.

'Good God, man! Are you mad?' The father ran to the doorway. 'Jethro! Send Mary to fetch warm water, bandage and iodine. Quickly, then take Matthias up to his room. You, miss, help him. I will fetch my bag.'

Matthias raised a hand to object, but as he did he swayed slightly. Between the servant, Jethro, Dorak and Sophie he was ushered to his room where Sophie stepped out as the two men saw to removing his clothes and placing him onto the bed. His father went to him with a black doctor's case in his hand. At a loss what to do and filled with concern for him she found herself in the corridor, waiting.

When his father returned she looked at him. 'He is a good man, sir. Whatever happened in the past, he has learned from his hurt. I think he is tired, but he is very lonely and you should not cast him off.' Sophie had surprised herself. She did not know the man and without Matthias there to protect her she could be thrown off the land.

'You speak boldly, miss. His last 'lady' he met on my friend's estate. She hooked him, turned his head, completely. He was lonely you see.' He paused, gathering his thoughts, his sadness plain to see. 'Then she ran off with a lieutenant, due to return to England.' He shook his head. 'Like a fool he followed them, going to ask her why. They were found murdered. He discovered their bodies. It was he who was dragged back to the barracks accused of reaping revenge for her betrayal. It was only by chance that a party of the new 'goons',' he paused and smiled at her confusion. 'The dragoons had found the bushranger's with the lieutenant's belongings still on him. That saved his life. He had already felt the lash, though. He should have let the calculating wench go.' He moved closer to her, his face flushed slightly. 'He still blames himself because she ran away. I never did.' He looked earnestly at her. 'Now, you come to my library, where we will have refreshments and you can tell me where that fool collected that bang on his head, along with a governess and a aboriginal boy who obviously has ministered to his wound and possibly saved the idiot's life.' He stepped back so that she could pass. She wanted to stay with Matthias, but knew that he was being tended well and that rest was what he truly needed.

She entered the library and looked at the man in front of her. There was a strong resemblance between father and son. Her instinct told her he was not the ogre she feared he was. Whilst he ordered a tray to be brought to them, she began to tell him the truth. It was a risk, but if she was not honest with him, how could she stay under his roof on whatever terms and gain his respect. Once she had finished, food and drink were there for her to have.

'I am Joshua Wells. I came here twenty years ago. Matthias was left at home to fulfil his education and then he was bought a commission. He has had a very different life to me. We were united a few years back, and have worked solidly here since. Until Beatrice entered his life and made a fool of him, he was a very independent and able young man. So, Miss Dove, you have had a very eventful week. Have you lifted your skirts for him?'

She stood up and stared at the man straight. 'No, we have not been 'united' not that it is any of your business. I am not a 'concubine' and have not been any man's. Matthias means a great deal to me and I will stay with him if he still would like me to, but I will not be talked to in such a way by you!'

'Sit down. You have nowhere to go, and without my son you would be in yet more bother. Drink up your tea, it is not cheap so do not waste it. You will be here as my guest. I shall have a room made ready and when I have spoken to Matthias then, we will see if he will live under the same roof as his father, or if he is too full of his own shame to face his father on a daily basis.'

'You mean you would not turn him out?' she asked.

'He is my son. Women make fools of us. I would not let one come between me and my son.' He looked at her determinedly so that his words were not lost on her. 'It is he who has to learn to forgive himself, not me. I will see to it that bodily he is fit you, miss, will make sure that his mind and heart are also. Do this, and you and your shadow,' he nodded to the door where Dorak was standing just within sight, 'may stay. Come in and eat, boy. You saved his life. I am a man of medicine and I would have you teach me some of yours from the local flora and fauna.'

Dorak came forward. He was allowed to eat and drink from the tray. He obviously was wary, but as Joshua questioned him they fell into a relaxed conversation. Sophie was taken to a room where a hot tub had been prepared. She let her body slide into it and tipped her head back with her eyes closed, and melted into its warmth.

She felt the touch of his lips on hers before her eyes opened. He sat down on the floor next to the tub smiling at her as his finger played with the surface of the water. She could not help but laugh, the colour high in her cheeks, the warmth that surrounded her was nothing to the feeling inside as she looked at his face.

'That bandage quite suits you,' she said, looking at his head, which was crowned by a band of white. 'Your father loves you, Matthias. He does not want you to go. He does not see those people's deaths as your fault — neither should you.'

Matthias flicked the water from his finger. 'I know.'

'You should still be resting.'

'I know that too,' he whispered, his eyes looking through the water.

She brought her knees up tightly to her body. 'Go back to your own bed, Matthias. This is not right, it is not the right time for us to . . . and you know it,' she whispered back.

'I just wanted to make you a better offer than that of a governess.' He kneeled beside the tub.

'You want me to be your 'concubine'?' she asked brazenly, whilst still hugging her knees to her, resting her chin upon them as she stared into his eyes.

'No,' he said, placing a kiss on her lips. 'I want you to be my wife.' He raised one hand above the water and opened his fingers scattering rose petals. Matthias watched them floating on the surface, flicking them into a whirl with his finger. 'Just say, yes.'

'Yes . . . but' she replied as he stood up and began to walk away,

'Where are you going?' she asked.

'Back to bed . . . I have my answer and I have a lifetime to answer all of Sophie's 'buts'.' He blew her a kiss from the door, and she smiled, sinking down into the tub amongst her rose petals. She closed her eyes and allowed herself to enjoy her dreams in peace.

# THE END

CHLOE'S FRIEND

A PHOENIX RISES

ABIGAIL MOOR:
THE DARKEST DAWN

DISCOVERING ELLIE

TRUTH, LOVE AND LIES